The Realm

KIERA CHAREST

Copyright © 2018 Kiera Charest

ISBN-10: 1983778796
ISBN-13: 978-1983778797

To my friend Helene, who
inspired me

Prologue

Bats screeched up above the thick marshland. The swamp was completely covered in fog. A light rain fell from the heavens, drenching the land in endless water. Behind an ancient stone wall, the sounds of urgent whispers echoed hauntingly across the marsh.

"I assure you, boy, you will be rich beyond measure," one voice hissed.

"Yes, come, come. Listen to his lordship," echoed another.

"But L..." the boy started to protest.

"Shhh! Do not use my name!" the voice fired back urgently. "From now on you address me only as Lord Cromwell."

"But that is not your given name," the boy protested.

"Do not argue with us, lad!" the other lord shouted harshly. "Cromwell wishes you to call him so and you will! Now, are you with us or not?"

Cromwell whispered in the boy's ear, "Do not make his lordship angry, for he will kill you."

"Very well, I agree. I shall join you, my lord," the boy said reluctantly. Getting down on his knees, he continued, "I will serve you faithfully."

The noble smiled savagely, "Oh I hope you will, for you would not want your life to end so suddenly."

Chapter 1

The loud racket of the Great Hall buzzed around Peter, making his head ache. In the afternoon, the hall was at its busiest. Merchants came from far off towns to trade and sell goods in the kingdom of Aurum. Tumblers and minstrels came searching for work, the scribes wanted to read the daily schedule to him, and worst of all, his soldiers would come and bring him criminals to be hung or thrown into the dungeon.

Running a hand over his face, Peter summoned his steward closer.

"Yes, your lordship?" Godfrey asked, bending over in order to hear better.

"Godfrey, is there much left to do? This room is giving me quite a headache," Peter asked, raising his voice above the noise.

"No, my lord, not much longer. But if it pleases you, my lord, I shall summon the rest of the people back later," Godfrey replied.

Peter shook his head, "That is not necessary, Godfrey. I will finish here and be done."

"As your lordship wishes," the steward answered. Giving a slight bow, Godfrey returned to his post behind Peter.

"You may bring the next man forward," Peter shouted, gesturing to the people across the loud hall.

One of Peter's guards came to the front, pushing a ragged man to kneel before Peter's raised platform. The man practically fell and planted his face on the hard floor.

Peter frowned, this had been the fifth time today that his guards had brought forth peasants. "Guard, explain to me why you have brought a serf to grovel at my feet once again."

The guard bowed respectfully to Peter before answering, "My lord, this lowly man was caught stealing from your bountiful land."

Peter raised his eyebrows. It was quite common for a pheasant to sneak food from a lord's forest. "That is all, guard? Whatever has he stolen? It must be something great if you came to me with the man."

"Well, nothing now, my lord, for I simply placed it in your own Artillery," the guard responded, spreading his hands into a fan-like gesture.

"What did he try to steal?" Peter asked, his calm demeanor starting to crumble.

"A couple of rabbits from your lordship's forest territory," the guard responded, glaring at the serf below him.

Peter sighed and rested his chin on his hands. It was the same problem that occurred over and over again. The village people just couldn't seem to leave his forest prey at peace. He knew this serf was not the same man who had robbed him the last few times, for this peasant seemed younger. Rubbing his eyes with the back of his hands, Peter groaned. He hated to do this, but he had to place a firm iron fist on the situation. He had let the other men go with a warning but, since they weren't stopping, Peter would have to lock up a few.

"What shall I do with him, my lord?" the guard asked, breaking into Peter's thoughts.

Peter eyed the man carefully. His features detected no sign of pain or misery, only fear. Closing his eyes, Peter began, "You may throw him in the dungeon. He shall spend the next few days there."

"What!" the man suddenly burst out. "No, no, no! Your Greatness! Pray forgive me! I was only trying to provide for my family, please. Please! You must understand!"

Peter held up his hand, "I do not wish to do this to you, but I must, for the law is the law. In this law there is a punishment for thievery."

"But, Your Greatness! Your most high, exalted..."

"Silence fool!" the guard interrupted, slapping the serf's head. Then, without a warning, the man was lifted from the ground and carried towards the door, heading for the dungeon.

Peter buried his head in his hands once again. He hated sending people to his dungeon, especially when another family was involved. But Peter was a lord and the law was the law. According to the feudal system, he was above the serfs and could do what he wished with them. Peter shook his head. Eighteen was still too young to rule a stronghold, not to mention four strongholds, which were given to him as a prize for participating in the war against Morgana. Peter groaned, why was this so complicated? You would think after being a lord from the age of fifteen he could send a man to a dungeon or the gallows with no hesitation. But he couldn't. At least not without asking a few questions and waiting several minutes before giving his final answer.

"Lord Peter?"

Peter's head shot up and took notice of Godfrey bowing before him. "Rise. What is it Godfrey?"

"There is a man here from Queen Charlotte's castle. He wishes to speak with you immediately," the steward reported.

"Very well, send him to my solar, for I will speak with him alone."

"Yes, my lord." Bowing, Godfrey left Peter to detach himself from his other visitors.

Peter entered his solar and found Godfrey and the messenger exchanging worried looks. Taking notice of Peter, both men bowed respectfully. "Rise, both of you," Peter began. "Now, tell me, messenger, what news do you bring from Her Majesty."

"Urgent news, my lord," the messenger informed. "Her Majesty the Queen wishes you to make hast and come right away."

Panic clogged Peter's throat. Urgent news. Whatever could be the matter now? Hadn't they just settled the kingdom peacefully? Was there more trouble now after Charlotte's successful three year rule? What could possibly be wrong? All the people seemed to adore the strong, young queen. Sure, she was stern occasionally, but only when she needed to be. Who would dare threaten such a small, peaceful kingdom? Peter shook his troubling thoughts aside. Perhaps he was over reacting. Charlotte seemed to be able to handle any sort of mishap. "Do you know what the queen is dealing with, messenger? I hope it is nothing terrible," Peter asked, trying to convince himself it wasn't.

"I'm afraid I do not, my lord. Her Majesty only said to make sure you come quickly."

Peter nodded. If Charlotte needed something, he wanted to help. "Do not worry, for I will come straight away as Queen Charlotte wishes."

The messenger bowed, "Thank you, Lord Peter. May you live forever."

"Nonsense. Everyone knows I will die someday." Turning to Godfrey, Peter continued, "Take the messenger down to the gates and send him on his way."

"Of course, my lord," Godfrey bowed and started for the door, the messenger tagging along behind.

"Make hast," Peter shouted after them. "Inform Queen Charlotte that I will be their as fast as possible."

"Yes, my lord!" the messenger's voice echoed in the hall.

The second the echo died down, Peter started for his stables.

Chapter 2

Peter set off quickly, forcing his courser into a swift gallop. While on his way, he tried to imagine what sort of news Charlotte had in store. It either had to be important for his status as a future knight, or troublesome news. Otherwise, the queen wouldn't have sent for him. Peter knew many of the lords wished Charlotte would find a husband in order to have a more secure throne and, of course, an heir for the future. But the strong-willed queen was determined to prove them wrong. First, by refusing to find a husband and second, by taking issues into her own hands and settling them on her own.

Peter only hoped that this news had nothing to do with putting Charlotte's life in jeopardy. A sudden memory clouded Peter's mind. There he was, standing by King Philip's deathbed, sharing his final conversation with his beloved leader.

"Promise me… you'll look after my… daughter. Promise me," King Philip's words echoed in Peter's mind.

"I promise, my king," Peter had replied, sealing the vow. Tears started to fill his eyes again as he recalled the king's last words to him.

"Goodbye, my son."

After that, everything was blank in Peter's mind. Not until he started his training again and busied himself with his duties as a lord, did the empty crater fill with new life and energy. Energy to be able to train as a knight as hard as possible, determined to make his father, Lord Robert, and King Philip proud. Now, he was close to finishing. Perhaps a month or two from his ceremony.

Peter shot out of his reverie and saw Queen Charlotte's castle looming ahead. Urging his horse faster, Peter's heart began to pound harder. What if the queen was already in danger? What if she was on the verge of dying? He shook his head vigorously and galloped across the drawbridge, giving a quick word to the gatemen as he passed over. Handing his stallion to a couple of stable boys, Peter dashed up the Keep steps and barged into the dim entryway. A steward immediately rushed up to greet him. Judging by the steward's expression, he was quite worried. Bowing, the man burst into a spasm of talking. "Lord Peter! Oh, it is good to see you, my lord! Queen Charlotte is in such a terrible state. She's raving mad I tell you. Perhaps she will listen to your reasoning, for she is refusing every other lord's."

"Calm down, steward," Peter began, placing a hand on the man's shoulder. "Of course I will reason with her. But I cannot promise you anything, for she is quite stubborn."

"I agree, my lord," the steward replied. "But I must warn you to be cautious, for she is quite aggressive."

Peter nodded. He had learned the hard way how aggressive Charlotte could be when something was bothering her. "Do not worry, for I have seen the queen in similar states before. She is only stressed and will calm down eventually," he reassured.

"Of course, my lord."

"What is troubling our good queen?" Peter asked, concern filling every word he spoke.

"I do not know, for the lords do not inform me on such matters," the steward answered, shaking his head.

"Very well, I shall be off to find out then." Peter started towards the Great Hall.

"Be careful, my lord," the steward called after him.

Peter raised his hand in reassurance and continued down the dark hallway.

———————

Peter neared the Great Hall's entrance and saw the other lords of the council lined up against the wall; Lord Edmund, Lord Geoffrey, and the newest, Lord Morris. Each of the nobles stood with their heads bowed and their hands folded or behind their back. Maids stood behind the throne, each looking terrified. From where he stood, Peter caught sight of Charlotte upon her throne. She was richly decorated in garments suited perfectly for her rank and the glistening crown on top of her head added to her beauty. But the queen herself was a sore sight. Her eyes were closed and her fingers were pinching the bridge of her nose as if struggling to calm herself. Her head lay rested on her palm as she leaned against one of the throne's armrests.

Luna, one of the griffins, lay at her feet. The creature matched Charlotte's demeanor perfectly. The black griffin watched the other nobles through piercing green eyes that were narrowed into slits. The feathery tail swished angrily from side to side. Luna caught sight of Peter and let out a low growl, letting its fur stand on end. Charlotte's head snapped up and her sharp, green eyes settled on Peter. She nodded for him to enter. Taking a deep breath, he walked into the large room and came to stand next to Charlotte's throne. Luna let out a hiss and started towards him. Snapping her fingers, Charlotte ordered the creature back to its place by her feet. Bowing, Peter waited for Charlotte to speak.

When she did finally speak it was through a cool, agitated tone, "Lord Peter, thank you for coming. Pray forgive me for summoning you on such short notice."

Her words sliced into Peter. Used to her friendly, cheerful way of speaking to him, he knew something was bothering her. "No need to ask for forgiveness, great queen, I will always come when their seems to be trouble."

"And you wouldn't come if there wasn't any trouble?" she fired back, her green eyes glaring at him.

Taken aback by her response, Peter simply bowed lower and said, "Forgive me, my great queen, if I have insulted you in some way, for I did not mean to."

Charlotte didn't respond, only rested her head on her chin again and snaked her gaze around the room.

Lord Edmund stepped away from the wall and walked towards the throne. Giving a slight bow, he began, "My glorious, illustrious, gracious..."

"Enough!" Charlotte shouted, "Lord Edmund you must simply tell me what you have to say. Fancy words will not help your cause. Now tell me!"

Peter flinched as Charlotte's voice thundered around the hall. This was a force no one wished to reckon with right now.

Lord Edmund began again, "My queen, perhaps you may let Lord Peter rise and inform him of the situation and discussion we have just had," the noble advised calmly.

"I will tell him when to rise and inform him when I am ready," Charlotte hissed back.

Lord Edmund only nodded and went to stand by Lord Geoffrey once again.

Charlotte stood to her feet and held her hand out, "Rise, Lord Peter. You may take a stand by Lord Morris."

"Yes, your Majesty," Peter replied. Though he preferred to stand by the other lords, he dared not infuriate the queen more. Rising, he walked over to Morris, giving the young lord a curt nod. Morris nodded back and turned back to the queen.

Charlotte sat back down and began to speak, "Lord Peter, we have been informed that there were raids on my local villages."

"Wouldn't such raids be natural?" Peter asked, thinking of all the times he had dealt with similar issues.

"Not these raids, Lord Peter," Charlotte answered. "These raids weren't for money or any sort of valuable product. They were for weapons and armor."

Peter was startled. Normally the robbers and highwaymen were only interested in money and the like. But never such bulky items as weapons and armor. Peter continued to study Charlotte's expression. It was obvious she was troubled and suspicious. Charlotte's gaze locked onto him. After a brief moment of gazing at him through worried eyes, she turned and addressed the rest of the lords.

"My lords, it was an honor speaking with you. But now I must ask you to leave, for I must think about this matter alone."

Peter nodded and bowed along with the rest of the nobles. Lord Morris whipped past him and found Lord Geoffrey. "Why didn't she tell him?" the young noble asked Geoffrey in a whisper.

Before he could find out what Morris meant, Peter felt a tap on his shoulder. Whirling around he caught sight of Lord Edmund smiling at him. "Lord Edmund, it is good to see you. How are you faring?"

"Quite well, Lord Peter, quite well," the lord answered. Heading for the door, Edmund continued, "But I should be the one to ask how you are. How is your training coming along?"

"Well enough," Peter answered, catching up with the noble at the door. "Sir Randolph is an excellent knight. Although I think he would prefer me to be housed with him instead of at my own fortress."

"Ah yes, you have a rare situation, my lord. But do not worry, for soon you will become a knight."

"Lord Peter, come here for a moment," Charlotte's authoritative voice rang out.

Peter turned to see Charlotte watching him. "Of course, my great queen." Turning back to Lord Edmund he nodded, "I shall see you again, Lord Edmund. Good day."

"Yes, yes, our queen needs you." Then, winking, Lord Edmund whispered, "I would watch that mouth of yours, she upsets easily."

Peter gave a short laugh and nodded as Lord Edmund turned and walked out of the room. Taking a deep breath, Peter walked back across the Great Hall and came to stand across from Charlotte and Luna. "Your Majesty, you wished to speak with me. Is something wrong?"

Charlotte turned to her maids behind her, "Go ready my solar for my afternoon meal." One turned to leave and looked back at the other hesitant maid. "Both of you, out," Charlotte ordered coldly. Nodding, the maids rushed out of the room leaving Peter alone with the vexed queen.

Chapter 3

Peter nearly held his breath as Charlotte's gaze settled on him once again. Luna looked up at her owner and let out a low guttural sound. "Rise, Peter," Charlotte ordered.

Obeying, Peter noticed Charlotte had not added the 'lord' in front of his name. Looking up, he also observed that Charlotte's demeanor had changed to the complete opposite of what it was a few minutes ago. Her green eyes let off their usual sparkle when she was happy. Standing, she advanced towards him. Luna stood to follow until Charlotte pointed to the ground, ordering the griffin to stay. "Peter, it is so good to see you again. I take it your training is going well?" Charlotte's words came out in a cheerful way, unlike her harsh comments earlier.

Struck dumb, Peter stammered, "Er…yes…well…you see…I…um…" he trailed off and looked into Charlotte's emerald eyes. Her gaze showed no sign of the anger that she had just communicated. Confused, he finally managed to ask, "Charlotte, I simply cannot fathom how you can be angry one moment and calm the next. It is impossible."

Charlotte laughed, "Peter, confused as always. Must I always explain to you certain obvious things?"

"Well, yes. That would be helpful."

Shaking her head, Charlotte continued, "I was never mad at you, Peter. It was the other lords, especially Lord Morris."

"May I ask why you were so cross with him?" Peter inquired.

"When I spoke of the raidings, Lord Morris brought up the subject of marriage and the rest of them started to add to that. They said it would be best if I had a king to take such matters off my hands." Charlotte buried her head in her hands and bowed her head. "I hate it when they bring up that subject, just hate it."

Peter studied Charlotte. The job of running a kingdom was weighing down on her and the other lords weren't helping. Part of him wanted to agree with the nobles about a secure marriage, the other part wished to see Charlotte rule alone and freely. But most of his mind turned to Morris. Anger started to burn in him at the thought of the young lord. Morris was beginning to remind him of his father, Lord Francis. Meaning well, not noticing the pain he brought instead. Lifting Charlotte's head in his hand Peter said calmly, "I understand, Charlotte. Morris can be quite overbearing at times, but he means well. In the end, he is like me, just wanting to see the kingdom safe."

Charlotte turned away from him and shook her head, "No Peter, he's nothing like you. You don't push me to my limits or try to force me to do such things as taking a husband. You trust that I can do this alone."

"Yes, I do. Because I saw how protective you were in Vetitum Wood. Or when you battled Morgana, your own mother." Walking back up to her, Peter took Charlotte's hand, "You would do anything to protect your home."

Laughing bitterly, Charlotte said, "All except marriage, for I would find a way out of that and defeat whatever was coming alone." Looking down at her hand in Peter's she pulled away, "Now I suppose the others wish you to speak sense into me. They assume I will listen to you."

"Yes, that is probably what they expect," Peter sighed. "But I know I shall have no luck in the matter, for you are quite stubborn."

Charlotte laughed, "Yes, I suppose I am."

"But I have dealt with many robberies, I could help you with that."

"I dare say you could," Charlotte replied, nodding.

"Then, may I?"

"Yes, but before you begin, let us go up to my solar. We will be much more comfortable and I am certain my meal is ready."

"Very well, do as you wish, for you are the queen," Peter answered, raising his hands in mock surrender.

Charlotte smiled and shook her head. Snapping her fingers, she alerted Luna. "Luna, up to my solar. Come along." Obediently, the griffin stood and started for the door, with Peter and Charlotte close behind.

———

Charlotte followed Luna into the solar with Peter walking by her side. Luna's daughter, Ferox, lay by the hearth, sleeping. Walking over to the younger griffin, Luna laid down and began to doze off. A maid hurried in from the east end of the solar. Curtsying, she announced, "Your meal is ready, your highness."

"Thank you, Mary," Charlotte replied. Turning to Peter, she added, "I would like to inform you that his lordship, Lord Peter, is staying to discuss a few matters. Bring forth another serving so he can join me."

"Of course, my queen. Is there anything else I can get for you, your highness?" Mary asked.

"Not at the moment. Thank you for your attendance, Mary. Now go and prepare his lordship's meal."

Stealing a quick glance at Peter then at the griffins, Mary curtsied, "Of course, whatever your Majesty wishes." Then, with a quick curtsy to Peter, the maid hurried out without another word.

Charlotte walked over to her table by the fire and picked up a few berries, "Peter you needn't stand by the door, come in," she said, glancing at Peter's position.

"Thank you, Charlotte." Peter walked over to the table and stood behind his chair, staring into the coals and fingering his sword's hilt. Mary rushed back into the room, carrying a tray of venison and fruit. Setting the tray down, she placed it in front of Peter. Curtsying, Mary turned and slipped quietly over to the side of the room by the hearth.

Sitting at the table, Charlotte began, "Now Peter, you may tell me how I should stop my robberies."

Shaking his head, Peter replied, "Oh, yes, of course." He took his seat by her before continuing, "I would start with sending guards down to your numerous villages. Robbers are less likely to steal anything with castle guards patrolling the streets. Make sure to send out new dispatches, every day and night."

Charlotte popped the berries into her mouth and nodded, "I have given that some thought. Now that I hear you do the same, I shall."

Peter swallowed a slice of meat and turned once again to Charlotte, "Is there anything else you wish to tell me about?"

Charlotte put down the apple she was about to eat, "Yes, one more thing. I promise I won't keep you long, for I don't want to disturb your routine."

Peter shook his head, "No fear, Charlotte. You shouldn't worry over such things. I will stay as long as you wish me to."

Charlotte smiled. That is what she admired about him. He was always loyal to the throne and determined to do whatever was needed. Then, the strange news clouded her thoughts. She took a step towards the door, snapping her finger so that Luna and Ferox would follow. "Peter, let us escape this stuffy air, I'm craving some fresh air from the castle garden."

"As you wish, your Majesty." Peter stood up and followed Charlotte.

In the garden, Charlotte gave a sigh of comfort and took a seat on one of the stone benches by a large oak tree. Gesturing for Peter to sit next to her, she sighed again, "I love it out here. It makes me feel more at home than the stuffy, dreary room upstairs. I can't imagine ladies sitting up in such a place all day and not venturing out of doors."

"Yes, I suppose many women do spend most their time indoors," Peter observed. Then, nudging Charlotte playfully he added, "But I certainly do not see you doing such a thing, for you grew up in Vetitum Wood. You will never lose your fighting spirit."

Charlotte smiled, "I agree with you." Then, getting up suddenly she faced Peter, "But, Peter, that is not why I brought you out here."

"Why?" Peter asked.

"I needed to talk with you alone and away from my maidservants."

"What of exactly?" Peter said, getting up to join her.

"Of a rather suspicious matter. Concerning my maids."

Peter gave her his arm. Linking her arm with his, Charlotte continued, "This morning a few of my maids went into town for a traditional festival. While they were there, a stranger approached them and questioned them about me. He told them if they knew anything about my whereabouts or strange behavior to tell him."

Charlotte watched Peter's eyes flood with concern as they continued their stroll. "Did your maids say anything?"

Charlotte shook her head and shrugged, "No, they kept quiet, or at least that is what they told me."

Peter looked up into the blue sky then ahead of him, "They could be lying, for servants can say what they wish their masters to hear."

Narrowing her eyes, Charlotte answered, "They wouldn't dare. All of my servants know I am not fond of showing mercy if I find someone guilty." Shaking her head in disbelief, "But Mary was with them. I can't see her lying, not even if she wasn't the one who told the lie and I most certainly do not see her hiding anything from her mistress."

Peter unlinked his arm from her grasp and faced her, catching Charlotte in his arms, "Still Charlotte," he urged, "it is best to keep your eyes and ears open. If something happens, you want to be prepared."

Charlotte smiled, "Peter, do not worry so. I am cautious. But, I beg you, do not jump to any conclusions. If anything else raises suspicion, I will take action."

Peter shook her arms gently, "But Charlotte, you realize..."

Charlotte held up her hand, silencing him. "Nonsense, Peter. I think I will realize if there is a real problem, but for now I will only keep an eye out."

Sighing, Peter linked his arm through Charlotte's once again. "Very well. What of the other lords? Did you inform them of any of this?"

"Nothing but the robberies. Besides," Charlotte began, sitting on another bench, "I did not get a chance, since they were babbling about other matters." Grumbling, she continued, "When they finally did settle down, I had lost my temper completely and I didn't care to tell them. Also, Lord Morris would find a way to relate it to marriage."

At the mention of the other young lord, Peter muttered under his breath. Charlotte shook her head, she knew Peter hadn't gotten along very well with Lord Francis, Lord Morris' father. But what caused Peter and Morris to hate each other was another story she didn't know. Perhaps it went back to when they were younger. An argument or rise in power? Charlotte gestured for Peter to sit with her on the bench. She would have to ask Peter about it later. For now, she must focus on these strange happenings. A low growl came from Peter's side of the bench. Charlotte turned to see Ferox eyeing Peter suspiciously. The lively beast behaved much like her mother, Luna, and she wasn't afraid to show it. Hissing, Ferox advanced towards Peter. Instinctively, Peter's hand grabbed his sword's hilt. Charlotte placed a calming hand on Peter's shoulder and snapped her fingers, pointing to the ground. When the griffin hesitated, Charlotte gave her a commanding look, piercing the beast with her green gaze, "Be still, Ferox. It is fine." Charlotte averted her gaze back to Peter, "You needn't worry about her, she is just protective."

"Much like her mother," Peter said, nodding towards Luna, lying under a large willow tree.

"Yes. Loyal, trustworthy, and protective. The critical features I look for in a beast like this," Charlotte answered, stroking Ferox's head. Standing up, Charlotte added, "I won't keep you any longer, Peter, for I am sure you have things to do."

"Yes, I believe I do." Starting back towards the gate, Peter continued, "A few serfs can't seem to leave my estates at peace. I must get back before my guards decide what to do with them without my judgement." He spun around and faced Charlotte once again. Gripping Charlotte's arms he looked into her eyes with concern, "Just promise me you will inform me if anything is amiss."

"Of course I will," Charlotte reassured. "If anything comes of it, I will send for you."

Peter nodded and released her arms, "Good. Then, I will see you later on, Charlotte." With a final bow, he hurried towards the stables.

Charlotte snapped her fingers, calling the griffins to her side. Starting back to her room she caught a glimpse of Peter galloping towards his fortress. She had promised to keep him informed and she would. But, also, she promised herself she wouldn't worry quite yet, for she wasn't in any danger in her own fortress. But, deep down, an old instinct of hers seemed to spark, warning her to be on guard.

Chapter 4

Peter's heartbeat doubled as he fought off his opponent. It had been a long, tiring day and Peter was starting to grow tired from the heat and constant battling. Mustering every ounce of his remaining strength, he fought on. Swinging his sword towards his opponent, Peter started to wonder if the battle would ever end. His question was answered when his opponent jabbed his sword into Peter's shield, pulled back quickly and aimed a blow at Peter's legs. Tripping suddenly, Peter fell to his knees and raised his hands in surrender. "You win, sir," Peter announced, breathing heavily.

His opponent raised his visor, revealing Peter's instructor and knight, Sir Randolph.

"Very well, boy. But next time I wish to see you at your best. You will not become a knight until you master the art of swordsmanship."

"Yes, I know, Sir Randolph. It is just that I have a lot on my mind," Peter replied, sitting down on a nearby stool.

"Ah, yes. Your business affairs at your fortress. You must have much to go back to these days."

"No, sir. Something else," Peter corrected, wiping his sword down with a rag.

"Oh? And what might his lordship have in mind? A young lady perhaps?" Sir Randolph teased.

Peter felt heat rising to his cheeks. Quickly turning away he answered, "No, not exactly. Just the queen, for she has been troubled lately." The word 'troubled' seemed to fit more of Peter's state of mind. Even though it was yesterday that Charlotte had discussed the matter with him, something didn't settle right in his mind. He would reassure himself that Charlotte would stay true to her word and alert him when needed, but he still had misgivings. Some nagging thought would remind him to be on guard and to be cautious around other people, especially servants. It was the same feeling when Morgana's threat had hung over the English kingdom.

"Ah, the young queen. Well, I wouldn't worry so, Lord Peter, for she is quite capable of handling matters on her own," Sir Randolph reassured. "She has demonstrated that quite often."

Peter nodded, putting his newly cleaned sword in its sheath. "I suppose so, but I shall still keep my eyes open, for I don't want anything to threaten the kingdom once again. It has only been three years."

"I know, my lord. I cannot agree with you more," Sir Randolph replied, his head bowed. "It would be quite a shame if trouble came prancing around the corner."

Peter was about to reply when he heard the sounds of thundering hooves coming towards him. Turning, Peter caught sight of a messenger sitting astride a chestnut courser calling, "Lord Peter! Lord Peter!"

Peter already knew there was trouble before the messenger dismounted. Considering the messenger's urgent tone, the news was bad. The man sprinted up to Peter and Sir Randolph. Giving a polite nod to the knight, the messenger turned his attention to Peter. "Lord Peter, I have terrible news."

"What of?" Peter asked, his concern rising.

"Of Queen Charlotte," the messenger replied.

"Speak on," Peter urged.

"The queen, my lord, is gone."

Peter's heart nearly stopped. Gone? He had seen the queen only yesterday. No, it couldn't be true. Gulping back his fear, Peter asked hesitantly, "Do you know where Her Majesty is? Perhaps the queen has only gone to Vetitum Wood, for you know of Her Royal Majesty's connection with the wood."

"No, my lord. She has been gone ever since you left the castle."

"What?" Peter exclaimed. Peter's anger and frustration started to rise. Why hadn't they said anything to him? They knew he was the queen's closest friend. He knew Charlotte better than anyone. He might have been able to solve this immediately. "And yet no one found it sensible to alert me?" Peter went on, struggling to keep his anger in check.

"Forgive me, my lord, but it is not what you think," the messenger replied. "We thought perhaps that she was with you, for the second you left she disappeared. She has not been seen since. Many are speaking of you kidnapping her."

Peter could not contain his anger any more. Who would think such things? Him kidnapping the queen? Drawing his sword and pointing it at the messenger he shouted, "This is outrageous! I would never commit such a crime! Who speaks of such things?"

The messenger fell to his knees, hands in the air. "The other lords, your lordship. Of course many servants as well, but not me. You are too good to commit such an audacious crime. Pray, I beg of you, have mercy! I do not believe, my lord, you would do such a thing."

"Calm yourself, Lord Peter," Sir Randolph said, laying a comforting had on Peter's shoulder.

Taking a deep breath, Peter placed his sword back in its sheath and rubbed his temples. The messenger's news and accusations from the other nobles made Peter tremble with concern. He was horrified, of course, that many thought he was the culprit. But, if he wasn't the one, then who would do such a thing? The way the messenger had given the news made Peter worry even more. How could she just disappear? Charlotte was never found off guard and she always alerted someone when she left for the woods. There was only one possibility. Charlotte had been kidnapped by someone in her own castle.

Darkness surrounded Charlotte as she fiddled with the cord tied around her wrists. She had no idea where she was or who had brought her here. She had been heading back to her solar from the talk she had had with Peter when a hard object struck her unconscious. Everything was black after that.

A key rattled in the door's lock and Charlotte could feel her rage starting to bubble. Whoever was there was going to regret ever coming in. A guard stuck his head in and smiled. "I take it you are uncomfortable, my queen."

The way he said it put Charlotte on the defensive. She glared back at him through her sharp, green eyes. "What gives you the right to kidnap me? I have done nothing to you or anyone else."

The guard held up his hands in mock surrender, "Your Majesty, *I* did not kidnap you. The lord I serve did." He came into the small room and advanced towards her. Charlotte's anger spewed even more. Her stone walls of defense were intact permanently now, making her invincible. "You shall regret coming in here. The pompous lord you serve will pay a heavy price as well," she hissed.

The guard only clicked his tongue and continued to walk towards her, "Ah, there is the temper his lordship warned me about." He walked behind her and snapped the rope with a knife. Whirling around she faced him, "Why did you free me? Surely you know of my aggression towards strangers," she demanded harshly.

"Oh I have heard, my queen," putting the knife back in his sleeve, the guard continued, "But surely you must have a soft side."

"No, I am steel and my heart is stone," Charlotte replied evenly. Then, threatening him, she added, "I warn you, guard, if you do not watch yourself, I will kill you."

At first, judging by the guard's startled expression, Charlotte thought he would leave in a hurry. Then, apparently thinking better of it, he continued, "All women have a gentle, loving side."

Charlotte crossed her arms and planted her feet wide. Her height matched the guard's evenly, considering how short the man was. "I have never shown anyone affection or gentleness in my life and I don't ever intend to do so," she retorted.

"Ah, nonsense," the guard replied, sweeping his hand in front of him. "You shall, eventually." The guard walked to the other side of the room and surveyed her up and down. "You are quite a pretty thing though. I must confess I have never seen anything like you. His lordship wasn't jesting when he said how stunning you are."

Charlotte eyed him suspiciously. "You would be wise to hold your tongue, guard," she warned.

"And you, my beautiful queen, would be wise to let down your walls, for his lordship is expecting you to dine with him," the guard answered.

"Tell your thieving lord he may sup alone. I would rather starve," Charlotte replied heatedly.

The guard shrugged, "Very well. But do not say I didn't warn you. His lordship upsets easily and will punish you greatly."

"I don't care," Charlotte retorted, "He will pay in the end."

The guard gave a quick huff and spun on his heel, bolting the door shut.

Surveying the room, Charlotte saw no possible escape routes. There were no windows, causing the room to be dark. The only light came from a dim torch on the wall. The door was secured with a heavy, metal bolt and the walls were made of tightly packed stone. Charlotte sat back down on the chair. She hated to admit this. There was no way out. She was trapped.

Chapter 5

"But my lord," protested Godfrey as Peter hurried towards his stables.

"I have spoken already, Godfrey, and my word is final. I shall search for the queen myself and bring her home," Peter replied firmly.

When they reached the stables, Godfrey was still protesting against the decision. "Can I not send some of your trusted knights to find Her Majesty, my lord? You mustn't leave."

"No Godfrey," Peter said, gesturing for a stable boy to saddle his courser. "You know of the queen's suspicion and trust issues; she wouldn't believe such men. Even if they did claim to be sent from me and assure her they are there to bring her home. No, I intend to do this myself."

Still Godfrey went on, "But, my lord, if you leave you will be putting your strongholds in peril. What would become of them if they are laid under siege?"

"I will entrust you to take care of such situations while I am gone, Godfrey," Peter replied simply. "You know that when I am absent, you are in charge."

"But…"

"Hold!" Peter interrupted, signaling to the stable boy.

"Yes, my lord?" the boy asked.

"Bring me Draco, for he will come along," ordered Peter.

"The griffin, my lord?" the boy asked fearfully.

"Yes, the griffin. Make hast!" Peter demanded. The stable boy nodded and rushed out in search of Draco.

"My lord, won't you listen to reason…"

"Enough, Godfrey! No more of this nonsense!" Peter crossly berated.

Startled, Godfrey knelt down, "Forgive me, my lord, for I only worry for you and your status as a baron."

Gesturing for the steward to rise, Peter nodded, "I thank you for your concern, Godfrey, but I must do this. If I don't, we may not have a monarch on the throne."

"Is that all your lordship is concerned about?" Godfrey ventured.

Sighing, Peter went on, "The other nobles think that I have kidnapped the queen."

Shocked, Godfrey exclaimed, "Whyever would they think of such a ridiculous notion?"

"I was the last person to be seen with her. It is just an assumption," Peter confessed. Then, more firmly, he added, "But I aim to prove them wrong."

"Would that not raise more suspicion when *you* bring her back? Since they thought you kidnapped her."

"Not if the queen herself tells them. They would believe her."

"But, my lord, is this the only other thing you are concerned about? Finding the queen and proving the other nobles wrong?" Godfrey went on.

Peter walked over to his partially saddled horse, "No Godfrey. There is one other condition."

"Oh? What else would his lordship be after?"

"Three years ago I made a promise to the king upon his last hours. I promised I would keep his daughter safe and protect her from harm." Turning back to Godfrey he added, "That is the other reason why I must go. I am breaking my promise to the king if I don't."

"If you don't mind, my lord, I would think you would have known better than to make such a promise. It is dangerous."

"Many have said that, Godfrey. But I don't care. King Philip was dying, I had to. It was the last order he ever gave to me and I intend to follow through with it until my death." Peter swung the reigns over the stallion's head and positioned the bit inside its mouth.

"Oh, my lord, I was going to do that!"

Peter swung around to find the stable boy panting at the doorway, Draco standing behind the boy's legs.

"I am in a hurry, boy. That is all," Peter replied, stepping aside to let the boy tighten the reigns and saddle. "I must get going."

"Where does his lordship intend to look for the queen?" Godfrey asked, standing beside Peter.

"Into Vetitum Wood," Peter replied matter-of-factly.

"But, my lord!" cried Godfrey, "You cannot go there alone. I forbid it, for you shall never come back. Absolutely not. Someone must accompany you."

27

Peter stepped forward to take the reigns from the stable boy. "That will not be necessary, Godfrey. I have returned in one piece many times. One question though, good steward, who gives you the right to forbid me from going where I please? Surely you have not forgotten who is in command, Godfrey?"

Hanging his head, Godfrey responded, "No, my lord. You are allowed to go where you please."

"Good, now I must be going. The earlier I start the better, for I don't want to be caught in that wood by nightfall."

"Of course, my lord," Godfrey replied.

Peter swung himself up onto his courser. Reigns in hand, Peter kicked the stallion in the ribs and rode off towards Vetitum Wood, Draco following close behind.

A slight drizzle rained down from the heavens as Peter's steed trudged through the thick muck of Vetitum Wood. Mist rose up taller than the horse's head and Peter had to squint in order to see in front of him. The wood was eerily quiet except for an occasional bat screech. The smell of swamp and rotting logs contaminated the air, making Peter gag. The place certainly hadn't changed in three years.

Draco walked on ahead making content, guttural noises in his throat. The narrow pathway opened up to a large pool of water surrounded by thick brush and trees. Peter swung down from his mount as memories flooded his mind at the familiar sight. Three years ago he had come here in search of his lost falcon. While searching, he had encountered Argentum. Then, being wounded in a fight against the griffin, he'd met Charlotte. Feeling guilty about the wound, she had taken him home and healed his sliced forearm. From that moment onward, Peter had taken a particular liking to the fiesty, independent girl. And now, she was missing. Making the sudden uneasiness and concern fill him once again.

A sudden feeling of fur brought Peter back to the present. Draco was nuzzling Peter's hand and growling. Then, walking a short ways, Draco stopped and growled for Peter to follow. Peter tied his courser securely to a tree and followed the beast helplessly. As Draco led him farther and farther away into the woods, Peter noticed the trees starting to thin out and widen into a forest of pure, white, birch trees. "Alba Wood," Peter whispered as the familiar land brought back more memories. Then, the realization hit him. Draco was leading him to Charlotte's former home, Black-fire Wood. Hurrying on, he hoped that he would find Charlotte along the way or perhaps in her old home. Knowing many people wouldn't venture as far as Alba Wood, Black-fire Wood would make a perfect hiding place for the culprits. The terrain became more and more rocky and full of large elms. Peter knew he was close. Following the mossy trail, Peter found himself in front of the old stone wall. Moss and ivy covered the stone wall, giving the stone an ancient look. Taking a deep breath, Peter pushed aside the vines, revealing the narrow pathway into Charlotte's cavern. Draco entered first, screeching happily as he ran back to his old home. Peter followed.

When he reached the end, everything he expected to see was gone. There were no griffins, no blazing fires from the large pits, Charlotte's house was in ruins, and, most alarming of all, Charlotte was nowhere in sight. Disappointment filled Peter. He had begun to think that he might get lucky and find her. But, he had been a fool to think the culprits would hide the queen in such an obvious place as this. But what also disturbed him was the wreckage he saw within the cavern. Before, when Charlotte was here, griffins were everywhere in the cave. The fire would never go out, it would keep blazing through the night; and most importantly, Charlotte's cottage had always been neatly woven and pieced together. None of it had lain in ruins.

Peter trudged wearily back to Vetitum Wood where he had left his horse. Draco followed behind, tail hanging low as if he sensed Peter's disappointment. Untying the reigns from the tree, Peter walked his horse over to the pool for a quick drink before he left. He would have to start from the beginning again and return home with nothing to show for it. Peter's courser bobbed its head up and down and turned away from the water. Getting ready to swing up onto the stallion's back, Peter heard the snapping of twigs coming from the kingdom's direction. As Draco began to growl, Peter knew it wouldn't be Charlotte, for the griffin sensed when a familiar figure approached. Peter reached for his sword's hilt, ready to attack when necessary. The brush gave way and two boys no older than himself emerged from the undergrowth. Peter recognized them immediately as Morris and Simon. The two boys stopped in their tracks when they caught sight of Peter. Draco let out an enraged yowl and charged towards the squires. Both boys drew their swords quickly. "Draco, enough!" Peter shouted. Draco stopped and looked back at Peter. Peter pointed to the ground next to him, ordering the griffin to stand by his side. Draco obeyed.

"Lord Peter?" Simon asked, surprise covering his face.

Peter recovered his shock and responded, "Yes, it is I. But whatever do you think you and Lord Morris are doing here?"

Morris stepped forward, "Lord Peter, we were aware of Queen Charlotte's disappearance and have come to search for her."

"You have?" Peter ventured further, "And may I ask why you have come to look here?"

"Because this is the last place anyone would set foot in." Morris nodded to his surroundings, "This wretched place was the queen's former home. If she was not kidnapped, then perhaps she had abandoned Aurum and come to live here again."

Fury bubbled in Peter. What right did Morris have of accusing Charlotte of such a thing? Drawing his sword, Peter replied fiercely, "Do not speak of such things! The queen would never abandon Aurum. If she ever did bring up such an idea it would be the cause of your talk of marriage."

"Oh? Is it really so hard to ask Her Majesty to secure the kingdom's fate with a future ruler?" Morris taunted, drawing his sword with a smirk. "I care about Aurum just as much as you, Lord Peter."

Peter was finding it more and more difficult to control his anger. If Morris said one more word he feared he would be locked into a duel with the arrogant lord. Simon stepped in between him and Lord Morris and said calmly, "Let us not come to blows, for more important matters are at stake."

Peter sheathed his sword and Morris followed suit, grumbling as he did so.

"Now," Simon began, "Lord Peter, would you like to explain your reason for being in such a dreadful place?"

"Yes, do tell," Morris said, sarcastically. "When you really could be sitting on your throne in one of your many fortresses."

Simon looked to Peter, sharing a sign of apology for Morris' behavior. Shutting Morris out, Peter turned to Simon and replied, "I am searching for the queen as well. Her sudden disappearance concerns me greatly."

"As does everything she does," Morris muttered.

Ignoring Morris, Peter continued, "I assure you, nothing is around these parts. Not a trace, for I have looked."

Morris grunted and came to stand across from Peter, "Something tells me that is a lie."

"Dare you question my honor?" Peter exclaimed, his anger rising once again.

Simon shot Morris a glare and Peter a warning glance. "Don't, Peter, he wants to make you angry," Simon seemed to be saying as he exchanged a long stare with Peter. Then, referring to both of them, Simon said, "My lords, I beg you, do not start up again." Turning to Morris, Simon added, "Lord Morris, explain to me why we can't trust Lord Peter's report."

"He was the last person seen with the queen."

"And how does that affect your trust towards me?" Peter challenged.

"I predict you are hiding the queen and trying to rile up Her Majesty's subjects and the other lords and barons."

"I would say you, Lord Morris, have encouraged that assumption," Peter retorted.

"Oh? So you deny you did such a thing?" Morris taunted. "Why, I cannot trust you at all!"

"This is outrageous! I would never..."

Simon held up his hand, stopping Peter. "Lord Morris and Lord Peter, please. Enough," he pleaded.

Peter sighed and circled around the pool, rubbing his temples as he went. Draco followed him. Lord Morris was always the cause of his temper flaring. Morris seemed to be bent on making his life miserable. But why? What had he done? Peter used to look up to the older squire. But now, there was nothing to look to. Peter pointed to a large pine tree, ordering Draco to stay below it. The griffin walked over and lay against the tree, flicking his ears back and forth.

Walking back over to the other squires, Peter took a deep breath. He decided to start over and try to befriend

Morris once again. Forcing himself to remain calm, Peter began, "Lord Morris, the queen's disappearance is troubling for both of us." Nodding to Simon, he continued, "We all want what is best for our Aurum. So, I would be honored if you and Simon would join me tomorrow for another search."

Simon nodded his consent, "I would deeply appreciate your help, Lord Peter."

Peter shook his head, "Simon, you needn't call me 'my lord'. Simply Peter like long ago."

"Very well, Peter. As you wish," Simon answered. Then, turning to Morris asked, "Lord Morris?"

"Oh very well," Morris replied reluctantly. "I guess the more people help the better." Eyeing Peter he added, "I propose that this search be longer. Say, two or three days."

"Very well, I will not argue with that. The longer the search, the more likely we are to find Her Majesty."

"Where shall we start?" Morris demanded.

"Lake Maud around dawn," Peter answered.

Morris nodded, "Then it is settled. We shall all meet at Lake Maud in the morning."

"And take care to bring weapons such as a sword and dagger," Peter instructed. "We don't know what we shall encounter along the way."

Morris frowned, "Do you intend to order us around? I certainly do not take orders from someone younger than myself."

Before Peter could reply, Simon stepped in between them. "We should be going. Come, Lord Morris." Hurrying the lord away, Simon waved a quick farewell and they both departed.

After they were gone, Peter surveyed his surroundings once more before swinging up onto his courser. "Come, Draco. We should be going as well." Riding back towards his fortress, Peter began to wonder where he and the others would begin their search. He didn't know the surrounding territories well enough to know where to look. Then, an idea started to form in his mind. He may not know the surroundings as well, but he knew of someone who might. The problem was, would he be able to give Peter the information he needed?

Chapter 6

Peter headed for Lord Edmund's fortress soon after leaving his own. After a quick explanation to Godfrey and leaving Draco in the stable boy's hands, he had set out for the other noble's fortress. While he was riding, Peter began to wonder if Lord Edmund would have the answers and information he needed. The older lord certainly knew the surrounding areas better; he could inform Peter on different places to look for Charlotte.

He neared Lord Edmund's gatehouse and watched as a guard came from the building. Reigning in his courser, Peter stopped and looked down at the guard. "Good day, guard. I am here to see his lordship, Lord Edmund," Peter announced.

"Who may I ask are you?" the guard asked.

"Lord Peter."

The guard bowed, "Forgive me for not recognizing you, my lord."

"You are forgiven. May I enter?"

The guard nodded, "Yes, you may." The guard waved a hand to the other guard near the drawbridge and shouted, "Lower the drawbridge!" The metal chains began to grate together, lowering the heavy, wooden bridge.

After a final nod to the guards and gatemen, Peter rode swiftly across. Tossing a stable boy his reigns, he jumped down and headed towards the Keep. When Peter entered the tower, he was met by a steward. "Greetings, Lord Peter!" the steward said cheerfully.

"You know me?" Peter asked, surprised.

"Yes, I was present in Her Royal Majesty's court when Lord Edmund was absent," the steward answered.

Peter nodded, "I see. His lordship is here, is he not?"

"Yes, yes, right this way," the steward replied, motioning for Peter to follow him.

———————

"Lord Peter! What an honor to have you under my roof! I must say, it is good to see you again so soon." Lord Edmund's greeting rang cheerfully through the Great Hall.

"It is good to see you too, Lord Edmund," Peter replied, bowing. "But I'm afraid this is not a social call, for I have a rather serious topic to discuss."

"Ah, of the queen's disappearance no doubt? Rise, Lord Peter, and tell me."

"Yes, precisely," Peter answered, getting up. "But, Lord Edmund, if I may, did Lord Morris ever accuse me of kidnapping the queen, for a messenger I saw said he did."

"Yes, he did," Lord Edmund responded, "But, Lord Peter, not many nobles agreed with such a possibility. Especially me, for you are much too noble for that."

"What of Lord Geoffrey?"

"No, he didn't agree with Lord Morris either. Only a few minor lords dared think that way. Do not fear, Lord Peter, Lord Geoffrey and I will always stand by you."

Peter breathed a sign of relief. It was comforting news to hear that these two powerful lords were by his side no matter what. He could trust them just like he had with King Philip. He shoved aside the thoughts of the former ruler. He refused to think of the king now. Not with Charlotte's sudden disappearance and, quite possibly, her life at stake. "Lord Edmund, I have many questions for you. Tomorrow I am planning a search party for the queen and I need your help on information."

"Very good," Lord Edmund praised. "You seem to have everything under control. How many people are accompanying you on your journey?"

"Lord Morris and Squire Simon. I fear I haven't spent much leisurely time with them since Morgana's defeat. I also feel that Lord Morris and I have grown apart lately. I must try to befriend him once again."

"Ah yes," Lord Edmund said, nodding, "A wise decision, Lord Peter.It is better to make peace with your enemy than to start a battle." Getting up, the noble walked over to Peter and gestured to some chairs by the wall. "Come, let us sit and talk." When they were seated, Lord Edmund asked, "Now, what are some of your questions?"

"I would like to be informed on the surrounding territories. The culprits could be anywhere."

"Yes, anywhere," Lord Edmund echoed. "You have already searched through Vetitum Wood, have you not?"

"Yes, along with Alba Wood and Black-fire Wood," Peter answered.

Lord Edmund nodded, "It seems uncanny that the culprits would take the queen far, for they probably plan to use her as bait."

"So you say it is dangerous to pursue them?" Peter asked. Without waiting for an answer, he continued, "But I must! They have our queen."

Lord Edmund held up his hand, "Calm yourself, Lord Peter. I know you care much for the queen. That is obvious to us all. But it is too dangerous to send you out. You must send some of your knights instead."

Peter shook his head, "No, Lord Edmund, I must do this myself."

Sighing, Lord Edmund remarked, "I can't stop you, just like I couldn't stop your father from carrying on with some things. I assume I must help you the best I can then."

"Yes, you must. Now, where shall the others and I search?"

"There is one place I can think of where you might look," Lord Edmund said, leaning back in his chair.

"Yes?" Peter pressed.

"It is called Malum Wood. Known to be a very sinister and dark place. But be mindful, Lord Peter, for I have heard of whole armies disappearing in that wood, with no trace left of them."

"Lord Edmund, have you been there yourself?" Peter ventured.

"No, I haven't. Only to Lake Maud near Vetitum Wood."

"I see," Peter answered, trying to hide his disappointment. "Then you have only heard stories."

"Yes, but some are true," Lord Edmund added quickly. "King Philip has even been mentioned in a few."

The mention of the former king caught Peter's attention. "King Philip?"

"Yes."

"Pray tell me of such a story Lord Edmund."

Nodding, the older lord began, "It is said that King Philip used Malum Wood as a place of banishment. He is said to have banished many former lords there, even Queen Morgana."

"Then it is possible to survive, for Queen Morgana came back, did she not?" Peter questioned, leaning back against his chair.

"Yes, but I still think it is madness to send you there, Lord Peter. You may very well perish."

"I know, but it is worth the risk." Peter answered. Then, amused he added, "You said you couldn't stop me. Am I right, Lord Edmund?"

"Yes, yes, you're right. I did say that," Lord Edmund answered. "Now, what other questions do you have for me?"

"Do you know of anyone who would use servants as a means of getting what he wants?"

"Why of course!" Lord Edmund exclaimed.

"Who?" Peter asked eagerly. Leaning forward, he waited for Lord Edmund to answer.

"All of us," Lord Edmund replied. "We use servants to prepare our meals, fetch us supplies, return and send out messages, and many more things."

"No, that is not what I meant," Peter put in hurriedly. "I mean as a way of spying and receiving vital information to find an opponent's weak spot."

"Such as? Give me an example, Lord Peter," Lord Edmund frowned, raising his hand to stroke his beard.

"I will tell you about something that occurred yesterday," Peter responded. "Her Majesty was informed of news that someone had urged her maidservants to give him any information concerning Her Royal Highness. Is that a common means of spying, Lord Edmund?"

The other noble's face went rigid. His eyes displayed a look of fear, dread and remembrance. "You said this is true, did you not?"

"Yes," Peter answered, wondering what was on the lord's mind.

"There is only one noble I know of that would have the nerve to do such a thing. But he has long been forgotten."

"Who, Lord Edmund," Peter pressed again.

"One by the name of Lord Tybalt."

"Lord Tybalt?" Peter asked puzzled, "I don't recall such a name in the king's court."

"No, Lord Peter. His lordship, Lord Tybalt was banished from the country long before you and Queen Charlotte were born."

"May I ask why his lordship was banished?"

"An assassination attempt," Lord Edmund answered. "Evidence showed that Lord Tybalt was to blame. King Philip ordered his lordship to be executed. But, before they could commence with the execution, Lord Tybalt escaped, never to be heard or seen since."

Peter shuddered. While Lord Edmund was telling the story, an idea was forming in Peter's mind. He just might know of someone to find more answers. But this time, the questions might be impossible to receive the answer to.

———————

"My lord! To what privilege do I owe such a visit?" the guard asked bowing respectfully.

Peter stared at his dungeon entrance. The wooden door was full of mildew and the hinges were rusty. The smell coming from behind the door made him nauseous and the dampness made him feel wet and uncomfortable. Peter took a deep breath, the sooner he got this over with the better. "Are we still keeping that man prisoner?"

"You have many men in your dungeon, my lord. Which one are you referring to?"

"The man that was sent down there recently. He was charged with stealing food from my woods."

"Ah, yes, that one. We do, my lord."

Peter nodded, "Take me to him."

———————

Darkness covered everything. The only light came from the torch on the wall. Water leaked from the ceiling, splattering across the cold, stone floor. In one of the mossy corners, Rowan sat slumped against the wall, struggling to catch some sleep. Last night, the rats would not leave him in peace. They always scurried about, stealing food or trying to bite him. No matter how hard he tried to block their way, the rats kept coming.

His stomach rumbled, reminding him of his hunger and the bruises on his arms reminded him of his last tussle with the guard. He got up and paced around his cell. He wouldn't be in this position if he hadn't made that deal with that evil, thieving lord. Now, instead of being at home enjoying his wife's cooking and seeing his beloved children, he was here in Lord Peter's dungeon. "All of this for stupid money and power," he grumbled to himself. He should never have made that deal. Even if the lord promised power and riches, it was wrong. He should never have agreed to betray his landlord, Lord Peter and help overthrow the kingdom of Aurum. He had a family to support and he could not do that from behind bars. He vowed he would try to get out of this as quickly as possible and go back to his family.

The heavy metal and wooden door swung open loudly and the same guard who had beaten him yesterday emerged. Rowan backed away and pressed against the wall of his cell, putting as much space between him and the man as possible. There was no telling what this guard would do next. The guard stopped before his cell and grumbled, "You have a visitor."

Rowan watched dumbfounded as he saw a man bedecked in the finest linen Europe could offer. Silver was decorated elaborately on his boots and doublet, sparkling as he walked in front of the dim torchlight. The noble's sword hilt was solid gold, delicately decorated with beautiful patterns. The lord surveyed him with dark blue eyes and a serious face. Rowan fell to his knees in respect and fright. There was no doubt about it. The man standing in front of him was his landlord. "Lord Peter," he said, "May you live forever."

Lord Peter frowned and turned to the guard. "This is the man. You may go."

The guard gave the noble a quizzical glance, "But, my lord, should I not stay here for your protection?"

"Why? The man is caged like an animal. What could he do?" Lord Peter challenged.

"Very well. But I insist that I stand by the door, for you never know what these serfs are capable of."

Rowan flinched as the guard spat out his rank. He could at least be grateful that the guard was not his landlord.

"Fine," Lord Peter replied reluctantly.

The guard walked over and leaned against the strong door. Rowan flicked his gaze back to Lord Peter. His landlord was approaching his cell. Rowan pressed closer to the wall.

"Come closer," Lord Peter ordered.

"As your lordship wishes," Rowan replied. He cautiously walked up to the cell's door and fell back on his knees and bowed his head. "Why has your lordship come to see me?" he asked, careful of every word he chose. This man had more power in one finger than he had in his entire body. He could easily send Rowan to his death.

"I will ask the questions," Lord Peter answered harshly.

Rowan bowed his head in regret. He should never have spoken. Glancing up at his landlord, Rowan noticed him rubbing his temples and closing his eyes. Being able to see Lord Peter up close in person, Rowan realized how young the noble was. He had always assumed he was older, perhaps in his thirties. Even when he saw him from afar his landlord looked older. Now, looking at him closely, he noticed Lord Peter was no more than a boy. A wave of sympathy rushed over him. This young noble had so much responsibility resting on his youthful shoulders. Poor lad, Rowan would do whatever was wished of him, no matter how bad it was. He would try to make his landlord's life a little easier.

Lord Peter sighed, "I apologize for my temper. Something is weighing heavily on my mind." The young noble's blue gaze blazed on Rowan once again. "Something *you* are a part of."

Rowan's heart began to pick up speed. What could his lordship want? Lord Peter's eyes still blazed at him like blue tongues of fire. "What does his lordship have in mind?"

"The queen."

Now, Rowan's heart nearly stopped. He forced himself to remain calm and to continue to make eye contact with Lord Peter. "I beg your pardon, my lord?"

"The queen is missing."

So, his evil lordship's plan had worked. Instead of feeling satisfaction like the evil lord had predicted, Rowan felt utter shame and guilt. Again he struggled to conceal his composure. "I never heard of such a thing, my lord," he lied, trying his best to look surprised.

"Oh? Have you not?" Lord Peter questioned skeptically.

"He isn't convinced," Rowan thought, panic starting to rise in his chest.

Lord Peter paced about the outside of the cell. Turning back to Rowan, he said, "We shall see how much you really know."

Fear replaced panic as Rowan stole a glance at the torture machines beside the wall. The hangman's nose seemed to grow in size and call out to him menacingly. He dragged his eyes back to Lord Peter and touched his head to the ground, "My lord and highest..."

"Don't waste my time with flattery," Lord Peter interrupted sharply. "I'm going to ask you questions and you are to answer truthfully. Is that clear?"

"Yes, my lord." He meant it. He didn't care whether the evil lord was betrayed. He preferred to help Lord Peter. If he gave his young landlord the answers he wanted then perhaps he would allow him to return to his family. Right now, he would much rather have his cottage in the village than money and power.

"Do you know of a Lord Tybalt?"

Rowan looked up at Lord Peter in surprise. The question was abrupt and the noble got straight to his point. "Er...yes, my lord."

"Any idea of his location?"

Rowan shook his head, "No, my lord."

"You lie," Lord Peter said, anger apparent in his voice.

"I do not," Rowan pleaded, "Lord Peter with all truthfulness, I do not know where Lord Tybalt is."

"If you know him, then you must know where he lies."

"I do not," Rowan repeated. "I haven't even seen him. I have only seen his henchmen."

"Who?"

"Pardon?"

"Who are his henchmen?" Lord Peter asked again.

"I only know of one."

"Tell me."

"A Lord Cromwell."

Lord Peter gave him a long stare then turned away, "You are lying. I have no memory of such a lord."

"But I speak the truth!" Rowan protested, throwing himself on the ground once again. Suddenly, he felt himself confessing everything to Lord Peter. "Lord Cromwell is Lord

Tybalt's new henchman along with a boy, whom I have never met. Long ago, Lord Tybalt persuaded me to help him figure out other nobles' weak spots. I was promised money and power in return for my service. Once I agreed, Lord Cromwell was placed over me and commanded me to find a way into your castle as a means of spying. That is why I stole your forest prey where your guards could see me." Rowan peered up at Lord Peter.

The young noble nodded, "Go on."

"I confess I found nothing that would be helpful to Lord Tybalt while I was down here."

"What sort of information were you searching for?"

"Information concerning the queen. Lord Cromwell said you are the young queen's closest friend. He was certain you would bring Her Majesty's downfall, my lord," Rowan stopped again, taking a deep breath.

"So you know of the queen's disappearance," Lord Peter observed.

"Yes."

"Do you know who was to kidnap her?"

"I do not. I only knew of my part in the plan."

"Final question."

"Yes, my lord?"

"Do you know where Lord Cromwell's hideout is, for he might be hiding the queen there?"

"Yes."

"Then where?"

"Malum Wood."

Rowan watched as Lord Peter's expression changed to one of horror. "My lord, are you well?" Rowan asked in concern.

"Not now. Not with Queen Charlotte's kingdom in peril."

Rowan watched his young landlord in sympathy. "Was I of much help, my lord?"

Lord Peter turned, "Yes," he blurted out. "Yes, you were. May I ask your name?"

"Rowan."

"Rowan, do you have a family?"

"Yes. A wife, a son, and a new baby girl," Rowan answered, wondering where this was going.

"Would you like to return to them?"

Rowan could hardly believe his ears. He had thought Lord Peter would release him at some point. But so soon? He was surprised. "Er...yes, my lord," he stammered, "But I thought you would..."

Lord Peter held up his hand, "I have no desire to punish you or keep you prisoner. Your act of stealing was fully paid for in the cell. But I have a different way for you to pay for your betrayal to your kingdom."

Rowan gulped. It didn't take him long to figure out Lord Peter could be ruthless when it came to protecting Aurum and its queen. What would the price be? Surely not death? He had asked if he wanted to return to his family. He had said he didn't desire to punish him. "Yes, my lord?" he asked nervously.

"You will aid me in my search for the queen. You will become a servant in my household and accompany me on a three-day search for Her Majesty."

"I see, my lord," Rowan answered. He was too relieved to say more.

"You will inform me of any information you may have of Lord Tybalt or this Lord Cromwell. Understood?"

"Yes, I understand, my lord." Rowan bowed his head again and added, "I am your faithful servant. I promise to serve you well, my lord."

Lord Peter nodded. For the first time since he came, he saw the young noble smile. It disappeared almost instantly when he called, "Guard!"

"Yes, your lordship?" the guard asked, approaching Lord Peter.

"Release this man, for he is now my servant."

The guard gave Lord Peter a dubious look. Then, seeing the noble's commanding gaze, obeyed swiftly. Rowan stepped out of his cell and bowed deeply to his landlord and new master.

"Rise and follow me," Lord Peter said.

Rowan nodded and followed Lord Peter up the staircase towards his new life.

Chapter 7

Peter rode off the next morning towards Lake Maud, Rowan following close behind. Ever since their agreement, Peter had gotten along well with his new servant. As they neared the lake, Peter made out the vague appearances of Simon and Morris standing underneath a large willow tree.

"Are those the other young men you were speaking of, my lord?" Rowan asked, riding up next to Peter.

"Yes, Lord Morris and Squire Simon."

"Are they around your age as well?" Rowan asked.

"No, Lord Morris is older and Simon is younger," Peter replied, glancing at Rowan. He was younger than most of his servants in his fortress. His hair was a dirty blond, his eyes brown, along with tanned skin, signifying long hours of backbreaking work in the fields. In all his life in King Philip's castle and his own, Peter had never encountered anyone so easy to talk to. Just yesterday, Rowan was made his servant. But in that short time, Peter had found himself telling Rowan all about himself, more than he had to anyone, even Charlotte. "Rowan?"

"Yes, my lord?"

"May I ask your age?"

"I'm twenty-two, my lord."

Peter nodded. Maybe that's why he got along so well with his new servant. Rowan was much younger than any of Peter's other servants.

"And you, my lord?"

Peter looked back over to Rowan, "Pardon?"

"If you don't mind me asking, my lord, but what is your age? I always expected you to be older, perhaps in your thirties."

Peter laughed, "I'm eighteen. It must be quite a surprise to find out such a fact."

"Yes, my lord. But, I must say I'm glad you are younger. You're easier to talk to."

"I must say the same for you," Peter replied.

As they drew nearer to Simon and Morris, Peter could see the two other squires mounted on coursers and each carrying a sword.

"May I ask your lordship one more question?"

Peter glanced at Morris and Simon approaching them. "One more."

"How long have you been given this position of authority, my lord?"

"Since I was fifteen," Peter answered.

If Rowan was surprised earlier you wouldn't have been able to tell next to his surprise to this other fact. His eyes and face showed a sudden wonder like that of a child receiving a gift.

"Well, you have arrived at last, Lord Peter."

Peter turned to see Morris approaching on his brown courser, while Simon followed on a chestnut stallion.

"Yes, we have," Peter answered.

"Who is this?" Morris asked, nodding to Rowan.

"My new servant," Peter answered, riding up to stand by Simon.

"You didn't say we could bring our servants," Morris said, frowning at Rowan.

"You didn't ask," Peter retorted. "Besides I didn't think you took orders from someone younger than yourself."

Before Morris could reply, Simon butted in, "We should be going. Peter, where shall we start?"

Peter turned to Rowan, "Earlier you spoke of a different wood beyond Her Majesty's territory. Are you certain that is a good place to start?"

"Yes, my lord. Malum Wood is..."

"Hold!" Morris interrupted. "Since when do servants inform lords on where to go? We go where we please."

Peter shoved his irritation down and replied calmly, "Lord Morris, Rowan was a spy for the enemy before he came to be in my services. He would know of the best places."

"A spy for the enemy!" Lord Morris exclaimed, "Why should we trust him at all?"

"You can trust him because I trust him," Peter responded evenly.

Morris just grunted and eyed Rowan suspiciously.

"Well, I think it is a pleasure to have you along," Simon said, turning to Rowan. "Thank you for your help on finding the queen."

"My pleasure," Rowan answered awkwardly.

Peter nodded towards Vetitum Wood, "Shall we go?"

The haunting squawking of crows filled the dark, starless night. Wind howled eerily through the gnarled, bare trees. The smell of dry, dead leaves swirled around Peter as he and Rowan urged their mounts onward. Simon and Morris looked around warily from the back. "This place is... enchanting," Simon muttered sarcastically.

"Mm," Morris grunted back.

Turning his courser around, Peter advised, "Perhaps we should search for a place to bed down, for its rather dark to continue."

"Malum Wood is always dark. There is no light here," Rowan informed.

"Not ever?" Simon asked incredulously. "Surely there is light some hours."

"No. Only an occasional glimmer from the rising sun in the morning," Rowan answered sadly.

Peter surveyed the dark landscape. "We should stay the night here." He pointed to a tree that formed a canopy over a flat piece of land. "Look, we shall use that as our bed. If it rains we needn't worry, for the tree will block the water."

"Well spotted," Rowan congratulated.

"I suppose," Morris butted in, "come on."

The four of them swung down from the horses and trudged sleepily towards the tree. Tying his horse to a thick branch, Peter felt around for a place to rest. Finding a log, he slumped against it and gestured for Rowan to join him. "We've been riding through this place all day. Have you the slightest idea where we are?" Rowan glanced towards Simon and Morris who were lying on their backs close by. Peter patted him on his shoulder, "It is all right, my friend, they are asleep. You may talk to me freely now. But, still," Peter said, "I don't see why you're so reluctant to say much in their presence."

"I don't feel very comfortable surrounded by nobility, that is all," Rowan answered. "I'm used to common folk like myself."

Peter nodded, "I understand. Do not worry about such a thing, everything will be fine."

Rowan eyed Peter thoughtfully, "I should be saying those words to you, my lord. I have seen the way you are when you have the queen in mind. You grow tense and frustrated."

Peter examined Rowan. Rowan's eyes were observing him closely and were full of understanding. "She is the queen and my close friend," Peter said, "knowing she is in danger makes me angry."

"Why is that, my lord?"

Peter got up and rested his forehead against the tree, "Because three years ago I made a vow to her father, King Philip, to keep her safe and to protect her." Sitting back down he continued, "Rowan, I cannot bear to lose her and break my promise. You must tell me where we are."

Rowan lowered his head, "Lord Peter, I haven't told you this because there was no time. But I was blindfolded when I was brought here. I only know the forest by smell and Lord Cromwell by his voice."

Peter's hope sank even lower. His face must have betrayed him because Rowan patted him on the back reassuringly and said, "Do not look so, my lord. I will do my best to guide you through this dark place. I assure you, we will find Her Majesty and bring her back to her rightful home."

Peter laid down and looked up into the sky. The branches were laced thickly together, blotting out the sky. They creaked and moaned in agony when the wind let out sudden outbursts of anger. It seemed impossible to think they would ever find Charlotte in such a terrible place. But, if Rowan's words were true and he could really navigate just by the smell and sense of the wood, then Peter knew they had a chance. He just hoped they weren't too late.

———

Hunger. Food. Starving. Charlotte tossed fitfully around on the prickly straw in her prison room. She had refused to dine with the lord who held her here against her will. In doing so, she was only supplied with enough food and water to survive. Why didn't they just let her starve? What were they waiting for? Surely they aimed to kill her? Rage boiled in her so hot and flaming she felt like she was turning into a furnace of hate. She had only felt like this long ago when she lived in Vetitum Wood. That was when she was young and everything she had was stolen from her. It was before she had the griffins, or the cavern, and before she met Peter. A sudden flicker of hope started to push past her anger and hatred towards her culprits. Peter. Peter must have known what had happened to her by now. He must be searching for her. He would never let her down. If she needed to be rescued, it would be from him and no one else. She felt herself drift into a more peaceful sleep, hoping help was on the way.

Chapter 8

Peter woke to the sounds of screeching bats fluttering around him. He sat up promptly and swatted at the pests, sending one crashing into the undergrowth. Getting up, Peter blinked his eyes, adjusting them to the darkness. Finally able to make out his surroundings, he walked over to his courser. He scattered more angry bats as he went. His courser snorted and tossed its head nervously. Calming his stallion, Peter knelt down by the horse's front legs and felt around for any bat bites. Sure enough, he felt the sticky substance of blood dripping down the courser's legs. Quickly, Peter took out his dagger and cut a piece of fabric from his shirt. Wrapping the strip tightly around the horse's legs, he stood up. After checking the rest of the courser's legs, Peter felt around the ground for his doublet. Finding it beside the log where he slept, Peter pulled it over his arms and hooked it securely together.

This was the last day of the search and so far there was no sign of Charlotte. Looking from the four horses to the three other sleeping men, a realization hit him. Perhaps they were making too much noise? It was possible. Four men traveling on horses could cause quite a racket. They might have frightened their enemy farther into the woods. After several minutes of debating, Peter decided to stake out alone on foot. He might get lucky and find Charlotte along the way. He started towards the thick undergrowth, then stopped. Peter looked back over his shoulder at his sleeping companions. Morris would probably find a way to accuse him for doing this alone. But it was a risk he was going to have to take. Charlotte was in danger; she was more important.

Trudging through the dark undergrowth, Peter blinked several times to adjust his eyes to the dark. A crow called eerily in the distance and bats squeaked continuously in the branches. Suddenly, a tree root caught ahold of Peter's boot, sending him tumbling into a mossy, stone wall. Pushing himself up into a seated position, Peter checked for a sprain. To his relief there was none.

Through the darkness, he caught the sounds of distant voices coming from behind the wall. Hoisting himself up, Peter pressed his ear to the stone and tried to make out what the voices were saying. The words were in a soft, whispering voice and were hard to comprehend. Until he heard the word, 'queen' did Peter realize these must be some of Lord Tybalt's men. Peter felt around for a crack or opening that he could put his eye or ear through. It was no use, he couldn't find a single one. He walked silently beside the wall, fingering for a hole. These men were most likely guards and he didn't want to alert them. Finally, Peter found a crack big enough to catch glimpses of the men. There were two guards standing by the wall, speaking in hushed tones. Peter put his ear to the crack and deciphered what they were saying.

"It is said that Lord Tybalt wishes to kill the queen," the first guard whispered.

Peter felt a shiver roll down his spine.

"Surely if he wishes to kill her it would have already been done," the second guard answered. "Why would he wait? She is of no use to him."

"Perhaps he intends to give her a chance to live," the first guard offered. "Possibly make her a serving maid in the castle. That would cause her great humiliation."

"No," the second guard said firmly, "if he let her live he would either marry her or keep her prisoner."

"Ah yes," the first guard answered, nodding his approval. "That would be an excellent set. The queen would surely agree to marriage over prison or death."

"Fool!" the first guard said harshly. "You have not seen what Her Majesty is like. She would rather rot in prison or die than marry some tyrant. She has vowed never to marry. I heard it with my own ears." The second guard shook his head, "Either way, his lordship must move fast if he wishes to take over Aurum, for surely there are already search parties out for Her Royal Highness."

Peter backed away from the stone wall as quietly as he could. His heart was beating fast and his mind swam with all the information he had heard. Silently, he headed back towards his group. He must tell them what he had discovered and devise a plan to rescue Charlotte.

Rowan paced back and forth impatiently, wondering what had happened to Lord Peter. Lord Morris and Simon were pacing to and fro as well.

"The longer we wait for Lord Peter the more time we lose," Lord Morris grumbled. I agreed to spend two full days searching and on the third and final day I would return to my fortress. I have much business to take care of.

"Perhaps I should go look for him," Simon suggested. "He couldn't have gotten far."

"No," Rowan said quickly. "You would get yourself lost as well."

"For once the servant is right," Morris said. "It's bad enough that Lord Peter has gone missing."

"But we have to do something," protested Simon.

"Would it not be better to leave Lord Peter to fend for himself?" suggested Morris. He's practically a knight, he can survive."

"Not if what Rowan says is true," Simon argued.

"Why are you so concerned about what a servant is telling you? They lie all the time," Morris retorted.

Rowan stood off to the side and watched the other nobles bicker. He couldn't bear to think about what might have happened to Lord Peter. His master had been his only friend who was nobility. He didn't want to lose such a friendship. The sound of running feet grabbed all of their attention. Rowan watched in amazement as Lord Peter stumbled into the clearing through the thick brush. The horses reared in fright and swung their heads. Lord Peter ran over to his jet black courser and stroked its neck, calming the nervous horse. Saddling the stallion, Lord Peter swung up and hastened over to them.

"Where in all the world have you been?" Lord Morris asked sharply, folding his arms, "I have much work to do today."

"We have to warn them!" Lord Peter burst out.

"What are you speaking about? Warn who?" Lord Morris asked.

"The other nobles, we have to warn them," Lord Peter repeated. He kicked his horse, hurrying it forward.

Simon ran in front of the stallion and stopped beside Lord Peter's saddle. "Hold, Peter. Just a moment. We are all full of confusion." Laying a hand on the courser's flank he continued, "Pray explain to us why you must warn the other nobles."

Sighing, Lord Peter swung down. Rowan could tell his master was impatient to be on his way. "I stumbled upon the culprit's fort early this morning. I got close enough to find out that they were holding Her Majesty prisoner there. Lord Tybalt is planning to kill her."

"You went on without us?" Lord Morris asked, eyes widening. "I thought this was supposed to be a group effort. Or perhaps you just wanted the glory for yourself," he spat.

"I only thought we could find more information if we sent out one person instead of a number of people and noisy animals," Lord Peter responded innocently.

"And it had to be you," Lord Morris spat back. "You could have shared the plan earlier with the rest of us and sent someone else out."

"Lord Morris, I am done arguing with you," Lord Peter replied, advancing towards the other lord. "We are wasting our time bickering. Now, I am going to inform the other lords about our situation." Turning on his heel, Lord Peter strode back over to his courser and swung up onto the stallion.

"You can't just barge into another noble's fortress unannounced," Lord Morris carried on. "You must be invited."

"Not if it is a matter of life and death. The queen's life is in grave danger and that calls for bending the rules."

"Do as you must," Simon said, nodding.

Lord Morris shot the younger squire a glare.

"Rowan!"

Rowan looked up at Lord Peter, "Yes, my lord?"

"Ready your horse. We must leave at once," Lord Peter ordered.

"Of course, my lord." Quickly, Rowan saddled his courser and swung onto its back. He trotted the horse over to Lord Peter's side and nodded, "I am ready."

Lord Peter turned his gaze to the others. "Are you coming?"

Simon nodded quickly and hoisted himself up onto his saddled stallion. Lord Morris followed, grumbling and shaking his head. As the group rode off, Rowan wondered what plan Lord Peter had for rescuing the queen. He just hoped whatever plan was forming in his master's young mind it would not be too dangerous.

Chapter 9

Darkness surrounded the damp tower. A dim torch shed its light across the floor, casting shadowy figures over the wall. In the small room, two cryptic figures stood across from each other. "Is what you say true? There are people searching for the queen?" one of the figures asked.

"Yes, it is true," the other answered.

"How could you let this happen?" the first man shouted back.

The second man fell to his knees and begged, "Lord Tybalt, please, do not be alarmed, for I know who is searching for Her Majesty."

"Who?" Lord Tybalt demanded.

"Lord Peter, Lord Morris and Squire Simon," the man answered.

"They are a threat to me. Kill them," Lord Tybalt hissed.

The man bowed his head, "I will do as you say. Lord Morris and Squire Simon shall be easy to take care of. It is Lord Peter I fear."

"Oh? You fear a lord no more than a boy, Lord Cromwell?" Lord Tybalt taunted.

"No!" Lord Cromwell said quickly. "It is just..."

"You will do as you're told," Lord Tybalt bellowed. "Or you shall not be rewarded."

Lord Cromwell bowed his head to the floor, "Yes, my lord and future king."

"Good. Is there any other news you wish to share?"

"One more thing, my lord," Lord Cromwell replied, rising to his feet.

"Speak on then," Lord Tybalt demanded.

"I forgot to mention one more man who is helping with the search for the queen."

"And who would that be?"

"A servant by the name of Rowan." Lord Cromwell winced and waited for Lord Tybalt to answer.

"What!" Lord Tybalt shouted furiously. Drawing a dagger from his belt he flung it against the wall. "Traitor! Traitor!"

Lord Cromwell fell to his knees in fright and watched helplessly as Lord Tybalt continued to bellow his rage against the servant.

"How dare he betray us! How could he? I promised him money and power! Money and power!" Lord Tybalt retrieved his dagger from the wall and brought it down against the hard floor. Seeing the angry noble bend down, Lord Cromwell saw his chance. Rising he backed away towards the door and said cautiously, "I am deeply sorry, my lord, I must be going, for I have some business to take care of."

Lord Tybalt stood up and whirled to face him, "You!" he shouted, pointing an accusing finger at Lord Cromwell.

Lord Cromwell stopped in his tracks, "Yes, my lord?" he said, noting the fear in his voice.

"I want those two lords, Peter and Morris, the squire, and that wretched servant dead within the morrow. If you don't do this quickly enough, I will kill you! Kill you I say!" Lord Tybalt berated harshly.

Lord Cromwell nodded hastily, "Very well, my lord, anything you wish."

Lord Tybalt continued, "Also I want Her Majesty dead! I have made a mistake keeping her this long! All of them! Dead! I will strike the kingdom when it is hopeless and unprepared. I will strike and bring it crumbling down to ashes!" Jerking his head towards the door, he demanded, "Go, now! Get out and do what you must!"

Chapter 10

Crows let out their mournful cry to the pitch black night. Peter crept through Malum Wood with his group of men. He had told Lord Edmund about his discoveries in the woods and the noble had supplied him with a couple of knights, Sir Henry and Sir Richard. Peter had brought along some help himself. He had asked his instructor, Sir Randolph to accompany him along with Morris and Simon, who had agreed to come. Silently walking up to the wall, Peter turned to the group. Through the darkness, Peter could tell the group was looking around warily. "What is the plan to get in, Lord Peter?" Sir Richard whispered, walking up to stand by Peter.

"I had the opportunity to observe the exterior of the fortress yesterday morning," Peter informed in a low whisper. "I noticed the fortress is not heavily guarded towards the back. While I was searching around, I stumbled upon an old wooden door. It appears to be a sally port. We could easily sneak in that way."

"Once we're inside what is the plan?" Simon asked.

"Lord Tybalt has many guards and soldiers," Peter informed. "I believe we can feign loyalty to him and act like his followers."

"Excellent," Sir Richard praised. "Only we must be careful not to look as if we are new and ignorant of the fortress. Also, we must not look like we are searching for anything," he warned.

"Then it is best to stay out of sight. Only encounter Lord Tybalt's men when necessary," whispered Sir Henry.

"It is settled," Peter said. "Act like one of them," he said, gesturing towards the wall. "But limit your appearance so they cannot identify you and tell Lord Tybalt."

Silent as ghosts, they continued through the dark night until they stood in front of an ancient wooden door. "That is quite a sally port," commented Sir Richard. "Usually they're smaller."

"I don't think it matters as long as we get in without being noticed," Morris whispered back confidently.

"Take care to be quiet, Lord Morris, we are near a door," Sir Randolph ordered in a sharp whisper.

Morris bowed his head in submission. Peter felt around for the handle he had seen earlier. Finding it, he opened the door a crack, taking care not to make noise. Peeking through he noticed two guards leaning against the opposite wall directly in front of him. Peter jumped back and held his breath, hoping the guards had not seen him. Peter caught sight of Simon picking up a few loose stones from the ground and tossing them at the far wall. The sound of the pebbles caught the guards' attention. The guards spoke a few words and turned to follow the noise. Seeing his chance, Peter bolted through the sally port and skirted across the bailey and into a dark corner. Seeing the others follow, he waved his hand to show where he was. "Quick thinking, Simon," Sir Randolph commented, nodding in approval.

Simon nodded back, "Thank you, sir."

"What's the plan? We can't exactly hide here forever," Morris said urgently.

"We should split up," Sir Randolph advised. "Lord Morris and Squire Simon will search in the west wing of the Keep. Sir Henry and Sir Richard will take the east wing." Jerking his head to the large tower, Sir Randolph added, "Go while you can."

"What of Lord Peter and you, sir?" Lord Morris asked.

Peter turned to his instructor, waiting for his orders. "We shall stand watch. If anything goes amiss we'll be ready to provide backup." Peter concealed his disappointment. He had wanted to help find Charlotte. Nothing could be more boring than waiting to be needed. But, he was a squire, he must do what was expected of him. And if he obeyed without issue and trained well, one day he would become a knight and be the one giving orders.

"Fair enough," Morris said.

Peter pushed down another wave of anger at the hint of smugness and approval in Morris' voice. He and Simon jogged towards the west wing, carefully staying inside the dark shadows. As he watched them go, Peter felt a tap on his shoulder. Turning he saw Sir Randolph smiling at him. "Lord Peter, go," his instructor said, pointing towards the Keep.

"Pardon?" Peter asked, confusion welling up inside him.

"Go find your queen."

"She's not my queen," Peter corrected, "she's our queen."

"Yes, but I do believe you are the only one who she shall wish to be rescued by."

Peter shrugged, "I don't know. Lord Morris will find a way to accuse me somehow. Plus, I am your squire, I do what is ordered of me."

"Well, I am ordering you to go and rescue your queen. Finding her is one thing, convincing her to follow is something I would think the others would find difficult," Sir Randolph said firmly. "And do not worry, I will deal with Lord Morris if he gives you grief." Sir Randolph jerked his head towards the Keep and ordered, "Go."

Charlotte woke and sat up promptly. There was mumbling outside her door. Charlotte put her defensive walls up and crept to a dark corner of the room. Drawing a hidden dagger from the folds of her skirt, she waited for her enemy to emerge.

"Who are you, young man?" the guard asked Peter as he walked up to a bolted door.

Peter cleared his throat and stood up straighter, "I am here to relieve you from your watch."

"You?" the guard asked in surprise, looking Peter up and down.

"Yes, Lord Tybalt's orders. He wishes to have his sturdiest men on watch on the flanking towers."

The guard shrugged, but then moved closer to Peter. "I would watch it, boy," the man whispered, "What's in there is a monster."

Peter feigned a scoff, "Oh come, come. It cannot be that bad."

"Why it is! And lower your voice, for she might hear you," the guard whispered urgently.

"You are afraid of women?" Peter asked amused.

"Only of that one," the guard said, pointing towards the bolted door. "If you value your life, do not go in there."

"May I look?" Peter asked.

"You'll regret it, boy. Trust me." Pulling up his sleeve, the guard revealed a long, red slice in his forearm. A memory flashed in Peter's mind at the sight of such a wound. He had been injured the same way when he first met Charlotte. She had agreed to fix it up and apply medicine to his wound. But Peter knew Charlotte wouldn't have apologized or offered to heal the wound on this man.

"Just to look," Peter pleaded. "My curiosity overpowers my want of safety."

"Oh very well," the guard said surrendering. Peter smiled at his sudden victory. This guard, whoever he was, was rather ignorant when it came to security. This would make him easier to fool.

———————

Charlotte heard the lock creak and the door open. Readying her dagger, she let her instincts take over. "You lied!" she heard a young voice exclaim. A boy around her age entered with a guard and looked around.

"I didn't! She is here. She must be," the guard said frantically.

The boy started to walk around, closer and closer to Charlotte's hiding spot. Her hand gripped her dagger. "Steady, my girl. Patience. Almost in range. Stay with your target," Charlotte's mind began to tell her.

"You lied, guard, for she is not here," the boy said.

"Hold!" Charlotte's mind ordered her hand. She knew that voice.

"But she is," the guard protested.

"Then where?" the boy challenged.

Charlotte's heart stopped. Peter. That's who it was. Peter. Relief washed over her. He was here. He was going to rescue her. Everything was going to be alright. "Oh stop," her mind scolded her, "Remain strong. You don't need anyone to rescue you. Especially a man." Taking a deep breath, she flung her dagger against the wall near the guard's head, drawing both men's attention. "Who's there?" the guard said nervously. Charlotte stepped out of the corner into the dim light, her green eyes blazing angrily at the two men. "What are you doing here?" she asked savagely.

"You see?" the guard said, picking up Charlotte's dagger. "She's a monster."

Charlotte winced as that word came out of the guard's mouth. She hated being referred to as something like that. But if it came to her safely, it was better to be fierce than vulnerable.

"I do see," Peter said, putting his chin in his hand and observing Charlotte up and down.

Charlotte remained firm and walked over to Peter. "Who are you?" she demanded harshly, hoping Peter would play along.

"Your Majesty, I am one of Lord Tybalt's new guards. I am going to be taking over this guard's shift." Peter walked over to the guard and teased, "You are afraid of her? What could she possibly do?"

"I could stab and kill you," Charlotte hissed savagely. She caught Peter's gaze and saw his blue eyes sparkle with amusement.

Peter walked around the guard and came to stand by the man's other shoulder. "I daresay, she is quite a beautiful young woman, do you not think so, guard?"

Charlotte's heart fluttered and her cheeks burned. This was the first time Peter had called her 'beautiful'. She shoved her rising feeling of affection down and frowned. "Hold your tongue you insolent boy!" she snapped.

"I was only complimenting you, Your Royal Highness," Peter replied, rising his hands in mock surrender.

Charlotte growled and stormed over to the opposite side of the room.

"Boy, we must leave at once. I do not trust her. She could explode any moment," the guard said nervously.

"Ah yes," Peter said, heading for the door, "and I don't believe Lord Tybalt is very forgiving when it comes to protecting his fortress."

"Ay! I forgot. Oh, his lordship will have my head in a noose if I don't..." the guard didn't bother to finish his sentence before he charged out the door, slamming it close accidentally.

Charlotte turned to Peter. He came towards her and whispered urgently, "Charlotte we must move quickly. This place is a deathtrap if we're caught here."

Charlotte remained firm, refusing to let her vulnerable side show. Even if he was her close friend, she still remained on her guard. "Very well, let us go." With her head held high she started for the door.

Peter stopped her and took her hand, "Charlotte are you well? You never act like this when your with me."

She sighed, "Peter I am only tired and hungry. I was only given enough food and water to stay alive. Then they stopped giving me those portions and today, thinking I was weak, attempted to kill me. I asked who ordered such an audacious crime and they answered that it was Lord Tybalt's wishes." She looked around the room then back into Peter's eyes, they were flooded with concern. "But I wouldn't have it, so I punished them. It was rather easy, considering I was more skilled at handling a blade than the murderers."

"I understand, Charlotte. Come, we shall return you to your rightful home."

"We?" Charlotte asked confused.

"Yes, I have come with a group. My instructor, Sir Randolph, Sir Henry and Richard, and Lord Morris and Squire Simon."

Shock ran through her. Why would Lord Morris want to help? He seemed only concerned about himself. The complete opposite of Peter.

"Why did..."

"Intruders!" a shout echoed down the dark hallway, causing both Charlotte and Peter to freeze.

"Now we really have to go," Peter whispered. Taking both her hands he added confidently, "Charlotte, I promise you, I will return you to your castle."

"Do not worry over a simple matter like that, Peter. I am quite capable of escaping myself."

Peter just nodded and gestured for Charlotte to follow him. Opening up the doors, they peeked out, making sure no one was around. Finding not a shadow, they hurried through the halls, down the dark staircase and hid behind corners. Suddenly a large brass bell tolled loudly across the fortress' territory. Charlotte ran faster, tripping on her gowns as she went. Growling under her breath, she wished for her leggings and tunic at a time like this. Quickly, Peter drew her into a dark corner and pressed her up against the wall. "Listen carefully, Charlotte," he whispered, his breath hot on her cheeks. "The sally port is right across from this corner. When the time comes, run towards the door. I'll be right behind you." The shouts of numerous guards clattered past them as they blended in with the shadows. "Have mercy, there are hundreds of them," Peter whispered.

The sound of running feet continued until it was quiet again. The only sounds coming from the outer bailey were the shouts of men battling against each other and the groans of agony from the slain.

"Peter," a whisper called urgently.

Charlotte peeked around the corner and saw Sir Randolph running towards them, his tunic splattered in blood. "Your Majesty! You are safe."

"I am," she replied.

"Where are the others?" Peter asked urgently.

"Sir Henry and Sir Richard are keeping Lord Tybalt's men occupied," Sir Randolph informed. "If you wish to escape, you must do so now, Your Highness."

"What of Simon and Morris?" Peter asked.

"I haven't seen them since I told them to search. I suspect they've been captured. We will have to come back with more men to make that rescue."

"They have the queen! She's gone! Catch them! Turn them over to Lord Tybalt! Kill them!" the guards' ranting bounced off the walls of the outer bailey.

"Get your men safely out of here, Sir Randolph," Charlotte ordered.

"What of you, Your Highness?" Sir Randolph asked concerned.

"Lord Peter will escort me out," she answered, turning to look at Peter. He nodded his consent.

"Then I will do what you wish, Your Royal Highness." Giving a swift bow, the knight was off.

"The sally port right in front of me, is that correct?" Charlotte whispered to Peter.

"Yes, once you turn the corner, you'll see it."

Charlotte nodded. Checking to make sure the guards were occupied, she bolted towards the wooden door. "Stop in the name of our future king!" a shout called. Charlotte turned around to see a guard running swiftly towards her. Feeling for her dagger, she realized the guard at her door had taken it from her. Now, she was defenseless. She heard a sword draw and in less than a second, Peter blocked the guard's way and attacked him with heavy blows.

"Keep going!" Peter ordered.

Charlotte took off again and swung open the sally port, slamming it behind her. Slipping through the woods, she disappeared into the darkness.

———————

Peter struck his opponent in the leg, sending the enemy tumbling to the ground. Quickly he knocked the guard unconscious with the flat part of his sword. Looking around, he saw Sir Henry and Sir Richard running towards him. "Where's Sir Randolph?" Peter asked, panic rising as he searched the dark landscape for his instructor.

"We got him out. We helped him jump the wall," Sir Henry answered, breathing heavily.

"Good," Peter said in relief.

"Now's our chance. Our enemy is confused. We either leave now or don't leave at all," Sir Richard said, taking deep gulps of air as he went. Through the dark, Peter could make out the signs of blood on Sir Richard's doublet. "It's my enemies'" he answered when he caught Peter looking at it in horror. Peter had just nodded and led the way out, but he knew that it was Sir Richard's life blood, draining as they trudged tiredly through the forest. "Where is Her Majesty?" Sir Henry asked after a while.

"I told her to keep going," Peter answered, "I haven't seen her since. I'm only hoping she didn't get caught, for it would be rather hard to sneak back inside Lord Tybalt's walls. He'll probably double his guards."

"No fear, Her Majesty is not caught," a voice informed, coming from ahead of them.

Peering through the darkness, Peter saw Sir Randolph and Charlotte emerge from the thick blackness. Relief washed over Peter like floodwaters to see the two most important people in his life safe. Walking over to Charlotte, he said formally, "Let us return you to your rightful home, Your Highness."

Chapter 11

Charlotte stood before her mirror and watched as one of her handmaids, Amity, dressed her. Flinging a long, white, linen tunic over Charlotte's head, Amity gestured for Charlotte to pull her arms through the wide sleeves. Obeying, Charlotte felt the fabric cover another shorter tunic she had put on earlier. The two clothing pieces were similar in design except the one she had just put on was longer, reaching all the way down to her feet, covering them. Amity took a white sash from her shoulder, bound the fabric tightly around Charlotte's chest and stomach, and ran lightly over to Charlotte's wardrobe. As her maid began to pick through Charlotte's numerous outer garments, Charlotte asked, "Amity?"

"Yes, my queen?" the young girl responded, looking up from inspecting a sapphire blue gown.

"After you have finished with this task, inform Mary to send out a messenger to the Lords of the Council," Charlotte ordered. "I wish to speak with them today."

"Yes, my royal mistress," Amity answered, giving a polite curtsy.

Charlotte nodded, "You may continue."

Amity turned back to the wardrobe and began to pick through the garments again, tossing aside countless gowns Charlotte would have preferred. Amity always saw it necessary to bedeck Charlotte in the finest fabrics Europe had to offer. While in contrast, Charlotte preferred a simple tunic and leggings, in which she could run unhindered. Her mind drifted from fashion to more severe matters. When Peter had brought Charlotte back to her fortress, she had decided right away that Lord Tybalt was a threat to her peaceful kingdom and her throne. That night, she had made up her mind that she would call upon the council members and discuss a plan to bring her rising enemy to justice.

"What does Your Majesty think of this one?" Amity asked suddenly, holding up a deep ruby gown, fit for a grand party.

"It does not matter today, as long as I am able to walk swiftly in such a piece of clothing," Charlotte answered, eyeing the bright gown up and down.

Amity sighed in defeat, "Well then," turning back to the wardrobe she pulled out a simple, pearl white dress and an ice-blue overtunic.

Charlotte nodded in agreement, "That is much better, I have no need for fine garments such as that other ridiculous gown."

Amity simply nodded and walked back over to her, head bowed in respect.

Charlotte leaned over, making it easier for the shorter girl to throw the pearl colored fabric over her head. "Your arms, my mistress," Amity said softy.

Sticking one arm out, Charlotte allowed Amity to pull the ice-colored overtunic through and rest the cloth on her shoulder. Once Amity did the same to Charlotte's other side, the maid skipped over to a finely-made pine chest, engraved with tiny sparrows. Opening the decorated box, Amity pulled out a silver satin cord. Walking back over to Charlotte, the maid wrapped it twice around Charlotte's waist and tied it loosely, letting the ends fall to Charlotte's feet. Charlotte's patience started to wear thin as Amity walked over to a golden-trimmed jewelry box and revealed a pair of diamond earrings and a sparkling diamond necklace. "I have no need for such delicacies," Charlotte thought as she groaned inwardly. But, she kept quiet, knowing she must look presentable when she met with the council later on. Adding the final touches, Amity stood back and looked at Charlotte with admiration. "You look...beautiful, my queen," the girl complimented shyly.

Charlotte only grunted and studied her reflection in the mirror. Her ice-blue outer garment was lined with a silver cloth on its ends and there was a slit through the middle, revealing her white gown underneath. Both garments touched the floor, hiding her feet. Her ebony hair flowed down her back to her waist. Her lips were dyed red and her piercing green eyes blazed back at her. The scent of lavender wafted around her and she noticed Amity had applied the sweet-smelling oil to her wrists and neck. She couldn't bear to look at herself dressed in such finery. Turning away she said softly, "Amity, this is too much. I look so..." Charlotte trailed off and walked around the room. She couldn't think of the right word.

"Beautiful and stunning," Amity answered, following Charlotte, she added, "You are the most beautiful woman in Aurum. Many see it."

Charlotte picked up the sweet tone of voice easily and eyed the maid skeptically, "Amity, where is this conversation leading?"

"Nowhere, my queen," Amity said quickly. "I was only trying to tell you, mistress, that you are radiant."

Charlotte nodded, "I don't like to be classed with beauty. I would much rather prefer compliments that involve strength and strategy."

"Yes, my queen," Amity said, bowing her head to look at the floor.

Charlotte gave a curt nod and replied, "We are done. Tell Mary to send out messengers. Make sure she tells the messengers that it is urgent."

"Your lordship's forest prey is finally at peace, for the culprits are decreasing daily," Godfrey informed as Peter strolled throughout his inner bailey. "Also, your auxiliaries are plentiful in case of an unexpected siege."

Peter only nodded and continued walking, his steward tagging along behind, still informing him on the daily news about his six other strongholds. His servants were running to and fro, obediently going about their orders. Many were too consumed in their work to notice when Peter walked by. Some would bow their heads respectfully then go back to their tasks. All the news, the bustling crowd, and his extensive training weighed heavily upon his thoughts. But what bothered him most was the thought of Lord Tybalt. All of this caused his head to throb. Peter rubbed his temples and started back to his Keep, hoping to catch some treasured silence.

"What would you're lordship prefer?" Godfrey asked suddenly, apparently asking his opinion of a subject his steward had just mentioned.

"Sorry, Godfrey, can you repeat that again? I was distracted."

Patiently Godfrey repeated what he had said, "The inhabitants of your countryside estate would like to know what goods should be shipped to your lordship for your table and trade."

"Tell them to send the ripest fruit and vegetation on the quickest route here. I..."

"My lord!"

Peter turned to see Rowan running from the gatehouse. Pausing beside Peter, Rowan bowed breathless after his run. "What is it, Rowan?" Peter asked.

"A messenger from the queen," Rowan answered through his intakes of breaths. "He is here to..."

"Lord Peter! My lord!"

Looking behind Rowan, Peter saw a messenger charging towards him. Rowan caught the frantic man in his arms and held him firmly by the shoulders, "Slow down, man, do not rush at his lordship like that."

"It's fine, Rowan." Nodding to the messenger, Peter ordered, "Speak."

"Her Majesty, Queen Charlotte, wishes to speak with the lord's of the council. She wishes you to come right away."

"I will," Peter answered. Turning around to Godfrey he added, "Godfrey, you may speak to me later about my fortresses."

Godfrey bowed his head, "Of course, my lord."

Turning back to the messenger, Peter ordered, "Go inform Her Majesty of my arrival."

The messenger gave a bow and ran off, jumping onto his horse and galloping out of the gates and across the moat.

"Rowan, tell a stable boy to ready my swiftest stallion."

Rowan nodded and took off towards the stables, calling for a stable boy as he went.

In less than a minute, Peter was galloping speedily towards Charlotte's castle.

Peter opened the Great Hall's doors and saw Charlotte sitting upon her throne. Looking around, he noticed that he was the first to arrive. Glancing back up at Charlotte, he saw her descend from her throne and walk over to him. Peter bowed with full veneration, "My queen," he said formerly.

"Rise, Peter," Charlotte said. As he stood up straight, he caught her gaze in his own. Her green eyes flashed with something he couldn't place. Her eyes revealed a distant look as if she was looking through him. He was about to ask, when, to his disappointment, she turned away from him and began to pace around the Hall.

In that moment, Peter took the time instead to study her. Her ebony hair flowed freely down to her hips, her eyes, of course, flashed with green, her lips red, and her frame encased in fine, white linen along with a light blue overcoat, decorated with shining silver hems and edges. He didn't have to think twice about his thoughts. She was beautiful. Now that he was older, his feelings for her grew harder and harder to hide. He came to realize a lot of nobles, especially Morris, seemed to notice his strange behavior or awed expression when she entered the room. He used to shove affectionate feelings behind him, not wanting anything to do with such time consuming activities. Whenever he began to feel that way, he would scold himself and force the feelings down, burying them under the weight of his work and training.

Suddenly, he caught Charlotte mumbling under her breath and fingering the silver cord tied around her waist. This, he knew, was a sign of nervousness. Just when he was about to ask Charlotte what was troubling her, the doors swung open and the two remaining lords walked in, accompanied by two servants.

"We apologize for taking so long, Your Majesty," Lord Edmund said, bowing.

"Yes, we are filled with guilt to think of keeping you waiting," Lord Geoffrey agreed, bowing next to Lord Edmund.

Charlotte replied in her usual firm way, "Rise. No need to apologize, my lords, I am in no hurry."

"Of course, Your Highness," they both answered.

Charlotte only nodded and went back to sit on her throne. "You lords are all aware of our new enemy and my escape, are you not?"

"Yes, my queen," Peter answered with the other two lords.

"I have decided to do exactly what I did with Queen Morgana," Charlotte began, "rid the kingdom of him permanently before he can do more damage."

"We are at your service, my queen," Lord Edmund responded.

Peter and Lord Geoffrey nodded their consent. They all knew it was of no use arguing with Charlotte about the matter. She was the queen and could do what she wished. "We must plan to attack Lord Tybalt's fort again. This time we shall have fully armed soldiers, knights, and siege weapons," Charlotte announced. "But first, before we plan a battle strategy, I must know all I can of Lord Tybalt." Turning to Lord Edmund she continued, "Lord Edmund, Lord Peter has told me much about our adversary and he informed me that you provided him with that information."

"Yes, that is true," Lord Edmund said, nodding.

"Is there any more information about this tyrant that I should know?" Charlotte asked.

Lord Edmund answered with a hint of fear in his voice, "The only other thing I can tell you is that Lord Tybalt is bloodthirsty. He will not let anything stand in his way. If something blocks his path to victory, he destroys it. He stops at nothing."

Peter felt a tremor of fear suddenly roll down his spine. This bloodthirsty noble was worse than Queen Morgana. If he was that determined to rule, he was going to be harder to get rid of. Peter could only hope that Charlotte had thought this through carefully and had a plan.

"I plan on taking a trip to town in order to find more information on Lord Tybalt," Charlotte said, rising from her chair. "I will disguise myself as a common peasant. That way, if there are spies around I will be less of a target."

"But surely you intend to have body guards along?" Lord Godfrey asked. Peter nodded, sharing the older lord's concern.

"Oh, of course," Charlotte reassured. "But they will stay at a distance in order not to raise suspicion."

Peter sighed with relief. There was nothing more important to him than Charlotte's safety.

"My queen, if I may, I have something you should know." Lord Edmund announced, approaching the platform and bowing.

"Rise," Charlotte ordered. "Yes, do tell me. I need all the information I am able to receive."

"Do you recall the prophecy of Queen Morgana, Your Highness?" Lord Edmund asked.

"Of course," Charlotte answered, "It was said that someone would have a certain dream and would rise up and defeat her."

"Correct, Your Majesty," Lord Edmund said, "There is a prophecy similar to that. It was engraved in stone long ago when Lord Tybalt was first banished. A woman gave us the stone, telling us we would not be free of Lord Tybalt's tyranny until these words were put to action and he was defeated."

Peter's mind was whirling. If all they needed to do was follow orders on a stone, Lord Tybalt would be easier to be rid of, wouldn't he? But, if it was just following advice engraved on a rock why didn't they conquer Lord Tybalt when he first disappeared?

"Where is this message?" Charlotte asked, pinning Lord Edmund with her stare. Peter knew she wouldn't believe something unless she saw proof. Lord Edmund gestured to one of the servants by the wall. The servant hobbled over to his master and handed him a heavy sac. Peter watched curiously as Lord Edmund pulled a thin granite stone from the sac. "I must warn you, my queen, it is not a clear message. It is written in the form of a riddle."

Peter watched for any sign of disappointment from Charlotte. Whether she was or not, she gave no sign. "I see. What is the riddle?" she asked.

Lord Edmund held the stone upward and began to read,

"If you wish to survive,
seek the fire in the ground.
Only then will you rise from the ashes
and defeat your foe."

After the riddle had been read, the room remained silent. Except for the words, that echoed across the Hall, bouncing off the walls. Peter turned to see Charlotte sitting on her throne unfazed by the message. At least, that is how she appeared. But, long ago, Peter had learned Charlotte hid a lot of her true feelings from people. Even from him. Leaning her chin on her hands, Charlotte looked around the room, then settled her gaze in the distance. After some time, she looked back at the lords and announced suddenly, "Thank you, Lord Edmund. In time, I assure you, I will find a way to decipher this riddle and bring Lord Tybalt's plans crashing down before him." Charlotte caught Peter's stare. Something in her eyes told him she was not telling the other lords her full plan. She rose and continued, "You are all dismissed. Now, if you'll excuse me I shall be starting for town immediately." With a final nod, she swept from the room, leaving Peter to wonder what else Charlotte had in mind.

Chapter 12

Peter headed for Charlotte's stables. Even though he was glad that Charlotte had a plan, he was rather annoyed when she didn't reveal the rest of it. The other nobles were content to go home and seemed to think Charlotte was telling them the full truth. But Peter knew her better. He always knew when she was hiding something. She would change into a calm and casual demeanor that fooled others well. Today she had done just that.

When Peter reached the stables a surprise awaited him. Charlotte was saddling Luna for flight. She had changed from her delicate linen gown to her simple navy blue outer tunic and brown leggings. Boots ran up to her knees and a small dagger along with a sword hung lazily from her waist. Taking a deep breath he stepped inside and approached her, "Charlotte."

Charlotte looked up and smiled, "Peter, you have arrived at last."

Taken aback by her comment he stared back in confusion. This girl could be awfully mystifying at times. "Yes, I have," he blurted out. "But, Charlotte why did you make such a comment? You never told me to come."

"Then why did you come?"

The question sounded more like a challenge. Her mood was shifting. "For my stallion, in order to go home," he answered, still unsure of where she was going with this.

Charlotte nodded, "That's what I thought. I knew I would find you here if I hurried. But it really wasn't necessary, considering how long it took you."

"Lord Geoffrey was visiting with me," he explained. Shaking his head, Peter said, "Never mind about that. What are you doing here? Did you need to ask me something?"

Charlotte got up and ordered Luna to stay before walking up to him. "Yes. But it is more of a request than a question."

"I will do anything you wish," Peter answered.

"Thank you. Now, Peter, listen carefully. I need you to come with me."

"Where?"

"To town, for information on Lord Tybalt."

Peter folded his arms and looked at her in puzzlement, "What makes you think the town has information?"

"Facts turn to rumors and rumors turn to town gossip," she replied matter-of-factly. "Word of mouth."

"And why do you want me to go? You will have body guards to keep you safe."

"Oh that." Charlotte turned away for a moment, then turned back, not daring to meet his gaze. He knew it. So she was hiding something. But, he was shocked at how she looked now. Normally she was an expert when it came to hiding her true feelings, but never had he seen her look so guilty.

"You lied?" Peter's question came out in a hushed tone.

"Not really. That is, if you come."

"But..."

"Peter, one person is better than having a huge army parading behind me. Your the only one I trust right now," she looked up at him with pleading eyes, "Please Peter, you must understand."

Peter gazed into her green eyes. For the first time in three years he saw real fear and worry in her. He sighed and pinched the bridge of his nose. He had made a vow to protect her and this might be the only way. But the promise was not the only reason to protect her anymore. His feelings for her were rising above the weight of training and work once again. He wanted to keep her safe because he was beginning to love her. He couldn't bear to see her disappear. She had said she trusted only him and he was beginning to think that was wise. He wasn't so sure it would be safe entrusting her to her bodyguards. Perhaps there was a spy among them? No, he couldn't trust anyone either. He wanted to be with her to keep her safe. How could he keep her secure if he stayed behind? No, he would go with her. Plus, he couldn't resist that beautiful, pleading gaze. "Very well, I will come. I want to keep you safe. I don't know what I would do if you..." he trailed off.

Charlotte's face was molded into confusion and shock. To his surprise, Peter noticed he was holding her tightly by the arms. Luna let out an enraged yowl. Peter released Charlotte quickly and raked a hand through his hair. "Forgive me, Charlotte. I didn't mean to..." he went quiet. Charlotte was looking at the floor and rubbing her arms where he had held her. "Forgive me," he said again. Then, he added softly, "Do you still wish for me to come?"

Charlotte let out a slow, wavering breathe and turned to Luna, who was still growling. Calming the griffin, Charlotte walked back over to him. Luna let out another angry yowl and followed her owner, hissing at Peter as she approached. Charlotte blocked the beast's path and said quietly, "Yes. I still want you to come. I need your help."

Peter nodded, "Then I will. I'm here for you, Charlotte."

Out of nowhere, Charlotte's mood shifted. She said in a firm, superior voice, "You will travel with me as my brother. But, do not tell anyone in your household about this. You must give the illusion that you are visiting another one of your strongholds."

"Of course. Why, may I ask?"

"So no other lord will grow suspicious and so Lord Tybalt doesn't see a weak spot. Oh, and of course, it is considered inappropriate for you to travel with me alone as a friend."

"I understand," Peter answered. She was right about all these things. Especially the latter reason. It would be dangerous to be found with the queen alone as a friend. But, as a brother, he would be much safer and she would be too. "How long do you plan to stay in town?"

"As long as it takes me to gather information on Lord Tybalt," Charlotte responded.

"You mean to leave today, correct?" Peter asked.

"Yes. One more thing."

"Yes?"

"Do not bring a horse, bring Draco and meet me near Lake Maud as soon as possible. We can't waste any time."

"Do you promise to keep everything organized and under control while I am away in the countryside?" Lord Peter asked Godfrey, as Rowan watched a stable boy prepare Draco.

"Yes, my lord. I assure you, I will keep everything in line while you are away," the steward answered.

Then, looking to Rowan, the steward added, "Rowan will be a great help while you are away."

Lord Peter turned from watching the stable boy and said firmly, "No, he will not."

Rowan was startled. Lord Peter hadn't spoken to him like that since they first met. Suddenly, his landlord smiled and patted Godfrey on the shoulder, "You can manage the estates without him, Godfrey. Rowan has a family to return to."

Rowan looked at Lord Peter in surprise. He knew Lord Peter would free him of his servitude eventually. But now? He'd thought Lord Peter would have him stay on until Lord Tybalt was taken care of. "You will allow me to go home?" Rowan asked, making sure he had heard Lord Peter correctly.

"Yes, Rowan. You may return home. But," Lord Peter added firmly, "You are still required by law to work for me in the fields."

Rowan nodded. Right now, he didn't care how much work was thrust upon him. He was too excited about going home to be with his family. What would his children think when he walked through the door? His wife was probably terrified right now. She was probably wondering what had become of him. "May I start out now?"

"You may," Lord Peter answered, walking over to Draco. Swinging onto the beast's back, his landlord looked from him to Godfrey and nodded. Kicking Draco lightly, the griffin tore off and flew through the air.

————————

Charlotte relaxed against a tree near Lake Maud, patiently waiting for Peter to arrive. A screech caused her to look up from her resting place. A distant image of a large bird-like figure was flying towards her, preparing to land. She noticed right away that it was Peter and Draco. Standing to her feet, Charlotte prepared to meet her travel companion. There was no one else she wished to have by her side in this troubling time.

Peter swung off Draco's back easily and trotted up to her, his sword swinging in its sheath by his side. "I'm ready, Charlotte," he announced. Then frowning, he asked, "Where is your griffin? You specifically said to bring the creature and you have none?"

"I did, Peter," Charlotte replied, "But I've decided we should walk to town in order not to frighten people away or raise suspicion."

"Where did you place them?"

"In my old cavern." She winced at the memory of her former home. Since she was queen, she was having difficulty looking after her treasured hideout. This was what caused the ruins she encountered when she dropped her griffins off. She shook her head, she could concern herself with decor later. Right now, her kingdom was in peril. She'd focus on that first. "Peter, wait here while I send Draco into Black-fire Wood. Once he is there he shall be fine."

Peter held up his hand, "There is no need for that. He knows the way from here." Leaning down, Charlotte observed in amazement as Peter gave a swift motion and pointed towards Vetitum Wood. With a screech, Draco took to the sky and disappeared into the forest.

"Was that admiration in her eyes?" Peter thought as he watched Charlotte observe Draco following his orders. Peter himself had to be impressed, for he had only taught Draco that motion a few days ago. But, Peter had learned that these beasts' were unbelievably smart and quick learners when it came to training. Even if they were swift to follow orders, Peter still couldn't wrap his head around how Charlotte had taught them everything from the beginning.

"How did you do that?"

Peter turned his sights from the sky to see Charlotte looking at him, her eyes sparkling with amazement and curiosity. "Extensive training every day. But, I am surprised as you are, for Draco only learned that command a few days ago."

Charlotte nodded, "If you don't mind, Peter, could you teach me?"

"Pardon?"

"Teach me how to give such a command. It will be useful one day for all my griffins."

"I don't mind at all, I would be honored to teach you."

Charlotte flashed him a quick smile before turning firm. "Peter, we should get started. The easiest route to town is through Vetitum Wood. If we want to reach it by nightfall we must move."

Peter simply nodded and followed after her. He still couldn't comprehend how quickly Charlotte's moods could change. He had begun to consider it being a habit she had picked up from living in Vetitum Wood. She seemed to possess many tones but he could only name a few. The first, he favored over all of them. It was a cheerful, content humor meant only for her closest friends. Another was her firm, no-nonsense, business-like tone she had when she conversed with the council members and gave orders. Then, last but not least was the mood Peter disliked the most, her angry mood. He couldn't understand why she possessed such a side. But possess it she did, for if anyone made her anger boil over they would feel her wrath. At times she turned violent and aggressive or lashed out ruthlessly with her tongue, creating threats that caused many people to consider their next move carefully before acting. Even though Peter had seen this state of mind at work only a few times, he still feared she would lash out at him unexpectedly. He never knew what Charlotte would do next. He had contemplated this angry temper and possibly knew what caused it. Some of it had to do with not being brought up with a governess at her heels, telling her whether to do this and not to do that. But most of her foul temper had to have been caused by past hurts and the lack of affection and love in her life. The more he thought about it, the more he was convinced the latter to be true. Her very own mother wanting to kill her was just one example. Was she ever shown affection in the past? His concern for her pressed him to know. Peter wanted to know what caused such bitterness. But would she tell him? Would she open her heart to him? Or would she push him away and block him out even more? Peter glanced her way. She was staring straight ahead, determination in every step. He had to at least try. "Charlotte?"

She turned to look at him, "Yes, Peter?"

Taking a deep breath, he hoped she would open up to him. "May I ask you a question?"

"You may."

"So far so good," Peter thought. "I have noticed, Charlotte, that you have many different moods. One in particular seems to disturb me." He held his breath. What would her reaction be?

Charlotte raised her eyebrows, "Oh? Which one would that be?"

"You can be rather aggressive when it comes to dealing with the council members and all the other nobility. You're never cheerful around them, either angry or firm and serious. Why is that?"

Charlotte's eyes seemed to portray a distant look. She seemed to be playing back a past event. Suddenly, her gaze turned sorrowful. She walked over to a dead tree stump and gestured for Peter to sit with her. "Charlotte, you don't have to answer if you don't want to. I won't press you for an answer. I want you to be able to tell me when you're ready. But, if you wish to talk now, don't worry, you can trust me."

Charlotte shook her head, "No, Peter. I can't keep this from you any longer." She drew a breath and began, "It was a past event that has caused me to have such a fearsome tone."

"Can you tell me what happened?" Peter asked softly.

"I don't remember much about my childhood. Only that when I was very young I lost my memory. I couldn't remember who I was or where my bloodline ran. I was taken in by a family in a nearby village. They were kind to me and cared for me like I was their own child. It was because of them that I know all I know today. The woman educated me in the healing arts. The older brother taught me to handle a blade. Lastly, the sister, who was my age, was the best friend I could ever have asked for. All was perfect, just how it was." Her eyes suddenly filled with tears. "Then, there was that dreadful day." She didn't say anymore. She leaned her head on her knees and remained that way.

Peter's heart ached for her. He wanted to comfort her the best he could. He reached out and softly laid a hand on her shoulder. "Charlotte," he whispered, "Please, can you tell me? I want to help."

She sat up with a start. Turning to him, her eyes hardened and her mood changed drastically. "They died. That's all," she replied flatly. "There's nothing you or anyone else can do." Swiftly, Charlotte got up and began to walk away.

Peter hurried after her, his mind still in shock on her sudden change of tone and what he had just heard. Charlotte lost her memory? That explained her reason for not remembering her royal bloodline or the escape to Vetitum Wood. She only remembered her child life in a small village. That meant she was raised by serfs. That alone was a lot for his mind to take in. Although he knew more of her past life, he still wondered what could have happened to her "family" and what might have happened if they were still alive. Charlotte would still be living with them and working long hours, not enjoying the royal life she had today. With all that information, she still hadn't answered his intended question. But he wouldn't press her. He would wait until she truly wanted him to know.

Suddenly up ahead Peter's ears caught the sound of a child's scream.

Chapter 13

The child's cry sounded again in the distance. Charlotte had heard it too and was looking around in concern. Peter started towards the sound with Charlotte following close behind. They hurried through the thick brush closer and closer to the desperate voice. As he neared a small open area in the woods, Peter noticed the crying coming from within. Peering through the tangled branches, he saw a small figure huddled on a rock, whimpering. He noted straight away it was a little boy. Peter stepped out into the opening and approached the child. When the boy saw Peter he cried out in horror and dashed into the nearest bush.

"What did you do?" Charlotte's voice sounded from the dense thicket Peter had come out of. Walking up to him, she looked at Peter for an explanation.

"Nothing. I was merely trying to approach him, but he got startled and ran into those bushes over yonder."

"Him?"

"Yes. It was a young boy. Possibly around three," Peter answered, recalling how tiny the child was.

Charlotte walked over to the bushes that Peter had indicated and pushed aside the brambles. Letting out a gasp, she waved Peter over. Curious to see what had startled her, he ran over. The boy was scratched and bleeding, his cheeks were streaked with tears, and his eyes were wet from endless crying. "Oh the poor child," Charlotte exclaimed in a soft whisper. In that instant, her tone changed into a voice Peter had never heard before. He watched in surprise as another temperament of Charlotte was revealed to him. "Come here, little one. We won't hurt you," she soothed gently. Beckoning the boy closer, she continued, "You must be from the nearby village. Are you lost? Come to me, dear. It is alright."

The boy crawled forward and was almost in Charlotte's arms when he noticed Peter and backed into the brush again, staring with wide eyes at Peter. Charlotte looked from the boy to Peter and shook her head. "Peter, perhaps if you stand back he will come out."

"Of course," Peter answered. He walked over to the rock and sat down to watch Charlotte at work.

"Now, now. Do not be afraid. He won't hurt you," she soothed. The boy began to crawl slowly towards Charlotte again. Charlotte kept on speaking in soothing tones, making Peter watch in amazement. He had never seen such a gentle and kind nature in the queen before. For once, Peter didn't know what to make of it.

Charlotte lifted the boy from his feet until he was wrapped in her arms. "Do you know where your mother is?" Charlotte asked gently, walking over to Peter. The little boy shrank back in her arms as she neared him. "There, there, Peter won't hurt you. There is nothing to fear," Charlotte reassured, rubbing the lad's back. "Where is your mother, child?" she asked again softly.

The boy whimpered and leaned his head on Charlotte's shoulder, still watching Peter nervously. Peter sighed, "Charlotte I think he is lost. He doesn't know."

"Yes, I suppose so." Then, pulling the child away to face her, she said, "Come, we'll take you home." The boy seemed to understand, because he nodded and laid his head on Charlotte's shoulder once again. "There is a village down this way," Charlotte informed Peter.

"How do you know?" Peter asked curiously.

Charlotte's voice clouded with grief, "I know because I used to live there. This village you will soon see is where I grew up."

When they came to a slope, Peter caught sight of Charlotte's childhood home. It was an ordinary serf's village, densely packed with small cottages, a stream ran through its center, and a large, stone cathedral stood proudly on the village Green.

The boy let out a sudden squeal of delight and squirmed in Charlotte's arms, trying to get down. Placing the child on his feet, Charlotte hurried to catch up with the running boy. Peter tagged along, concerning himself with keeping Charlotte and the boy in sight. In such a village he was helplessly lost. He grew up in a large castle; he had no knowledge of these outer villages, save for business matters. Abruptly, Charlotte stopped dead in her tracks. The boy was skipping happily towards a small cottage. The stream wrapped around half the house and made its way into the forest beyond. Peter walked up to stand by her side. "What is it, Charlotte?"

Her lips began to tremble and her eyes turned moist, "This cottage...I remember it so well. It's just how it used to be," she whispered. "This was my home before..." she trailed off and looked at Peter. Startled, she switched to her firm tone, evidently not intending him to overhear her whispered words. "Never mind, I wonder who owns the land now?"

"Gavin, my child! Where on earth have you been?" a woman's voice exclaimed from inside. There was a shuffle of feet and a flurry of motion from within the cottage. A woman in a simple dress with an apron tied around her waist stepped out of the doorway, a baby in her arms and the boy clinging to her skirt. Peter heard Charlotte take a deep breath and step over the stream to approach the woman. Peter followed suite.

"Thank you so much for bringing my son home safely," the woman said when they stood face to face.

"It is our pleasure," Charlotte answered formerly. "I am glad to see he is in safe hands once again."

The woman peered at Charlotte closely and looked her up and down. The woman's eyes widened in shock and she stepped back, putting a hand over her mouth.

"What is it?" Charlotte asked in confusion.

"Charlotte?" the woman asked in a whisper. "Is that really you?"

"How do you know my name?" Charlotte asked.

"You probably don't remember me. It's been so long. But I remember you as if it was only yesterday. I would recognize that firm voice anywhere."

"Who are you? How do you remember me?" Charlotte pressed.

"Charlotte, do you not know who I am? I'm Alice, your sister."

Peter stared at Charlotte and Alice in disbelief. There was no possible way the two women could be sisters. Then, he remembered Charlotte's story of her life in the village. She had said she lived with a serf family. This must be one of them. But Charlotte had told him they had died. Or was she hiding something from him?

"Alice?" Charlotte whispered in surprise. "No...It can't be..." she spluttered. "The fire...you died...you all died."

"No, Charlotte. I escaped the flames," Alice answered.

Charlotte was shaking her head in disbelief, tears brimming in her eyes.

"I never thought I would see you again," Alice whispered.

Charlotte nodded, tears started to fall from her eyes. She brushed them away quickly. Alice looked at Peter in puzzlement, "Who is this?"

Charlotte spun around and wiped her face, making sure to get all the tears away. Peter knew she was trying to hide the fact that she was crying in his presence. "I'm Peter, her brother," he lied. He had to stop himself from adding the 'lord' in front of his name.

"So you found an actual relative to live with after that day? I am so glad. I thought you lived in the woods until you died." Alice said, relief covering her features.

"Yes," Charlotte answered, "A true relative. But I'm afraid this is going to be hard for you to digest."

The baby in Alice's arms started to cry, making the mother bounce it up and down. "Perhaps you two should come inside," Alice said. Then, mock scolding, she told Charlotte, "You have a lot of explaining to do."

Charlotte laughed and they both followed Alice into the cottage.

Rowan stared at his cottage from across the stream. It was still intact, it was still perfect, it was still a comforting sight. Home. He was home at last! A cry of delight sounded from the cottage doorway. Rowan watched as his son, Gavin, came gallivanting towards him. Rowan crossed the stream in a single bound and knelt down, giving his boy a fierce hug.

"You're home!" Gavin said breathlessly.

"Yes, my boy. I'm home to stay." Rowan got up and watched Gavin bouncing in excitement. "Gavin, is your mother home?"

The boy bobbed his head in return and said, "And two more people. Mother said they are her friends. They brought me back home from Lord Peter's forest."

"And what do you think you were doing in his lordship's territory? Gavin, you know better than to wander off," Rowan scolded lightly.

"Mother will explain."

"No, you will explain the second we enter the house," Rowan said firmly.

Gavin sagged his head, "But I don't want to do it in front of people."

Rowan shook his head, "Fine, but you will explain some time. For now, I would like to meet your mother's friends and see your sister, Faye."

Gavin lit up with excitement again and pulled Rowan towards the cottage, "Come."

———————

When Rowan entered his cottage, shock overtook him. There, sitting in a chair by the fireside was his landlord. Another young woman sat next to him. "Rowan, my dear, you're home!" Rowan's gaze shifted to his wife, Alice, as he noticed her shoo Gavin onto a stool. Alice walked over to him and embraced him tightly. "I thought you would never come home. I told you that Lord Peter would lock you up. You know how vexed our landlord is when it comes to his forests. But, locking you up is a brutal punishment! I wish I could speak my mind to that arrogant noble we call our landlord." Rowan found Lord Peter watching in amusement. Instantly, it occurred to Rowan that Alice did not know their landlord was sitting under the exact same roof. "She must know the young woman," Rowan thought. "But what is Lord Peter doing here? Especially clothed like a villager? And who was the woman? A servant?"

The woman looked up at Rowan, revealing a piercing green gaze. Rowan's daughter, Faye, broke into cries from her cradle, causing Alice to rush over. The woman rose and continued to study Rowan. "This is your husband I presume, Alice?"

"Yes, Rowan." Alice said, picking up Faye, "and Rowan, this is my sister, Charlotte, whom I have told you much about. You do remember, correct?"

"Of course, my dear," Rowan answered. Lifting the young woman's hand, he placed a quick kiss on it and said formally, "I am honored to make your acquaintance, my lady. You must be a relative of Lord..." he trailed off when he saw Lord Peter quickly shake his head. In a flash, the woman pulled her hand away and her green eyes hardened. Strange.

Normally women adored such a gesture. But perhaps it was different in a noble society.

"I am pleased to make your acquaintance as well, Rowan," Charlotte replied firmly.

This was even more strange. Normally a woman would not answer in such a way, especially a servant. But then again, what did he know. He could be completely wrong. Rowan watched as Lord Peter whispered something to Charlotte. She nodded and bowed her head. Smiling, Lord Peter shook Rowan's hand, "Rowan, it is good to see you again. I take it you are happy to be home?"

"You know each other?" Alice asked, bouncing Faye up and down.

"Yes," Lord Peter replied, turning to Alice, "I do apologize for keeping him at my castle for so long, but I needed him to aid me in a... political issue."

Alice shrank to her knees in fright. "My lord! Lord Peter. You are his lordship?"

Lord Peter nodded, "Yes."

Alice shrank even lower, clutching Faye closer, "Forgive me, your mighty lordship for speaking so poorly of you. Please show mercy, I beg of you!"

Rowan waited to see what Lord Peter would do. Hopefully his landlord was not a noble who was offended easily.

"Rise. Do not look so frightened. I will show you great mercy and gratefulness. For your hospitality now and in the past, I will reward you and your family greatly when I return to my stronghold."

Alice rose and looked at Charlotte. "Charlotte, if Lord Peter is your brother then does that not make you a Lady?"

Charlotte took a deep breath, "No."

"No?" Rowan and Alice asked together.

"Alice, I lied to you. Lord Peter is not my brother or any relative. He is a friend."

Alice peered at Charlotte closely, "Then, if he is just your friend why..." her mouth twitched, "Charlotte are you..."

Rowan watched as Charlotte's eyes narrowed into slits and her cheeks flamed red. "No," she said firmly, "No, I am not."

"Then what connection do you have with Lord Peter?" Alice asked, looking from Charlotte to their landlord.

"Alice," Charlotte began slowly, "This will not be easy for you to hear, but you must, if this is to make any sense."

Alice nodded, "Go on."

"First, let me ask you a question," Charlotte said. "Who is the queen? Do you know Her Majesty's name?"

"Why of course!" Alice answered. "Queen Charlotte the First of Aurum, daughter of King Philip and Queen Morgana."

Rowan's thoughts froze when he saw Charlotte nod. He turned to see his wife in the same position. Alice was gaping and Rowan had to grasp her arm to prevent her from dropping little Faye and falling. He sank to the floor with Alice and stared at Lord Peter for an explanation.

His landlord nodded at him then looked to what Rowan now knew was the queen. Queen Charlotte was under his roof.

"Your Majesty," Alice whispered, "My queen, I had no..." she trailed off when she noticed Queen Charlotte's eyes narrow.

"You mustn't call me or Lord Peter by our noble status. We must blend into the community if we are to accomplish what we've come to do."

What they've come to do? Rowan was confused. But wasn't everyone? What was so important to bring the queen and his landlord to his cottage? Wasn't Lord Peter supposed to be in the countryside? Was any of this related to the current search for Lord Tybalt? He needed answers desperately to be able to comprehend what was occurring in the kingdom. He could see Alice was equally confused because of her puzzled expression.

Exchanging a glance with Lord Peter, the queen said, "We will explain."

Alice nodded and rose, "Very well. But first let us eat a fine supper, you two must be starved."

The queen nodded, "That would be fine."

"And please, spend the night here before carrying on with your journey, for you will not find a suitable inn for your status in many miles." Alice continued, handing Faye to Rowan.

"Thank you for your hospitality, Alice," Queen Charlotte responded, "I will take your kind offer and pay you for your trouble when I return home."

"It is finished, Lord Tybalt," Lord Cromwell announced triumphantly, "Lord Morris is dead."

"And the boy?" Lord Tybalt asked from the shadows. "You said you captured two the night the queen escaped from our grasp. Is he dead?"

Lord Cromwell nodded slowly, "Yes...yes he is. I have completed my orders."

Lord Tybalt smiled savagely, "Good. The time to strike is upon us. But first, you must complete one more task. There is one more lord I wish for you to kill."

"Name the noble and this shall be his last night," Lord Cromwell said, bowing his head, "I am at your service."

"Lord Peter. He is the one I want dead by sunrise."

"As you wish, my future king."

Chapter 14

Peter gave a long, satisfied sigh and stretched by the doorway of the small cottage. The morning was fresh and full of life. The rising sun cast its rays across the small village. Dew lay fresh on the ground, glistening like diamonds on the plants in Alice's garden. Birds sang cheerfully in the sky, carrying their joyful melody across the soft, blue sky. Inside, Charlotte and Alice were busy preparing breakfast. Gavin sat on the floor, entertaining baby Faye with straw horses. Rowan came to stand by Peter's side, "Lord...I mean...Peter, where do you intend to travel next?"

Peter looked back at Charlotte speaking to Alice by the boiling cauldron. "That is in the queen's hands. I go where she commands."

"I see," Rowan responded.

Peter turned back to study Charlotte. The day before she had explained everything and made it clear that she was in great haste to gather needed information on Lord Tybalt. Alice and Rowan had agreed to help her in any way they could. Faye began to whimper softly and tug at Alice's dress. Alice clicked her tongue, "Faye, must you always be in my arms?"

Charlotte laughed and stooped down to pick the babe up in her arms. Lifting Faye from the floor, she held the child close to her chest and began to hum softly in a sweet voice. It amazed Peter how the queen could have such a loving side. All through the years, Peter had seen Charlotte serious, firm, angry, and friendly, but never gentle and loving. Those two traits didn't seem to fit into Charlotte's character. But, then again, what did he know? Charlotte was certainly holding back some of her past from him. Perhaps if he grew closer to her she would open up to him.

"Peter?"

Peter turned to see Rowan watching him in amusement. Only then did he realize that he had been staring at Charlotte for far too long. Frustration started to build up in him. Fool! What was he thinking? He had let his stupid feelings rise again. He turned his gaze to the village, trying to make his voice casual, "Yes, Rowan?"

"Nothing, I was simply wondering why you were gawking at the queen," Rowan replied, smiling at Peter.

"Her actions surprise me sometimes," Peter answered quickly, wanting to finish this awkward conversation as swiftly as possible. "She's never been very gentle before. It shocked me, that's all."

"Ah, I see," Rowan answered. He said nothing more on the matter, which Peter was thankful for. It seemed that Rowan always knew when to drop a conversation. He never probed or teased Peter about a matter that was uncomfortable for him.

"Breakfast is ready," Alice announced from inside. "It's nothing very noble," she confessed shyly, looking from Peter to Charlotte.

Charlotte put a hand on Alice's shoulder, "If your mother, Ellyn, taught you to cook, then you could easily host many nobles."

After the humble breakfast, Peter let out a contented sigh, "Alice, Charlotte was correct, you have the makings of an excellent cook. I might consider hiring you for a few of my banquets."

Alice blushed and added with a shy smile, "Thank you, my lord."

Peter then turned his attention to Charlotte next to him. "Where do you intend to head next? I assume you have a plan?"

"I think I needn't worry about going anywhere. I thought it over long and hard last night and I think Rowan and Alice may be able to help me."

"How may we be of assistance, my queen?"

"It is not so much new information I need about Lord Tybalt, it is the rather complicated and puzzling riddle. If I can simply decipher what it means then it will instruct me on how to bring Lord Tybalt down."

"This riddle you speak of, what is it, my queen?" Rowan asked.

Charlotte studied Rowan through her critical green eyes as if wondering if she should trust him. After a few seconds she spoke, revealing the riddle, "It states, *'If you wish to survive, seek the fire in the ground. Only then will you rise from the ashes and defeat your foe.'*"

Rowan and Alice exchanged glances. Rowan leaned towards Peter, "My lord, I have heard of a certain fire that some say comes from the ground."

It was Peter's turn to lean forward, "Go on."

"There is a wood named Black-fire wood that contains this certain fire."

"Black-fire Wood?" Charlotte asked dubiously, "I never heard of that wood possessing fire. I used to live there, you must be mistaken, Rowan."

"Perhaps you did not explore fully, my queen. Black-fire is vast."

"Is that why the forest is given such a name?" Peter asked.

"Yes, and the name follows the legend of a creature that is said to roam those parts."

"Tell us of the legend," Charlotte said.

At the sound of the story, Gavin hopped up from his stool and climbed onto Rowan's knee, waiting eagerly for his father to start. "Long ago," Rowan began, "There was a bird larger than any eagle that ever lived. The feathers of this said creature were majestically painted with fiery red, orange, and blinding white. The feathers were so bright the large bird could be seen from miles away. This was a disadvantage for such a creature.

One day in the late spring, a hunter was out searching his traps for the prey he had caught the night before. Almost instantly, he caught sight of the bird. He was amazed at the bird's beauty and size. The bird looked like golden fire in flight and shone as brightly as the sun. The hunter decided to capture the creature and sell it to the wealthy nobleman for whom he worked. Using a netted crossbow, the hunter shot the magnificent bird from the sky and watched in triumph as it fell to the ground. But when the hunter reached the place where the bird lay, he was stricken with sudden horror. The net was burned into nothing but ashes and the ground surrounding the soot was burned with a mark resembling the bird itself. The hunter tried in vain to find the bird, but never saw the creature again.

A hundred years later, the hunter's descendant was netting prey when a flaming bird crossed his path. Like his greedy ancestor, the man tried to net the bird to sell. The same thing happened, except that this time the man witnessed the bird rise up in flames, turning the net to ash and burning a mark in the ground. The bird disappeared in an instant, never to be seen again. It is said that every hundred years the bird will come out of hiding and burn another mark in the earth." Rowan set Gavin on the floor and turned back to Peter and Charlotte, "That's the legend."

Normally, Peter stayed clear of such chimerical legends and mystical creatures. His father had never believed in anything of that nature and he made sure he drilled his beliefs into his son's mind. Peter looked to see Charlotte's reaction and was surprised to find a look of realization. "I think I may know what this prophecy means," she whispered. She jumped up promptly, sending her stool to the ground with a loud thud. Standing it back up, she turned to Alice, "Thank you greatly for your hospitality, Alice. But I am afraid we can stay no longer, for I must act quickly if I am to bring Lord Tybalt and his forces down."

"Of course. We understand," Alice replied, standing up. "It was really nice to see you again after all these years, Charlotte."

"Same to you, dear sister," Charlotte said, embracing Alice, "I promise to repay you when I return to my castle."

"Do you really have to go?"

Peter looked down to see Gavin staring up at him with pleading eyes. Peter chuckled and hoisted Gavin up into his arms. Ever since Alice had reassured Gavin that Peter and Charlotte were safe, the young boy had taken a particular liking to Peter. Since Lord Robert was never around Peter to set a proper example as a father and because of his strict living conditions with King Philip and his own fortress, Peter always felt awkward and nervous around children. But Gavin seemed to change all of that. One look into those big, eager, and happy eyes, Peter's awkwardness was forgotten. "Now, listen Gavin, I must do what is expected of me. I am in the queen's service."

Gavin hung his head.

Rowan ruffled his son's hair, "Don't you mope about, Gavin, you may see Lord Peter again."

Peter set the boy down, "That's correct. I will be back to reward your parents for their hospitality and I might consider giving you a surprise."

Gavin started to hop up and down, "What? What?"

Peter laughed at the boy's eagerness, "You shall find out soon enough. That is if you behave for your mother and do all that is expected of you."

Gavin bobbed his head, "Very well."

"Then you will find out in time."

———————

"Lord Tybalt, we have a problem."

"You mean to tell me *you* have a problem, Lord Cromwell?" the other noble's voice hissed through the damp, dark tower. "Everything that happens around here will never be my fault. The blame falls on your shoulders."

Lord Cromwell let out a wavering breath, "It is as you say, my lord," he said nervously.

"Good. Now, what problem have *you* created?"

"I have created none. Only that Lord Peter was not at his fortress when I requested an audience with him. They say he is in the countryside."

Lord Tybalt let out an evil snicker, "Fool. Leaving his property to be sieged."

"Do not underestimate that young lord," Lord Cromwell replied firmly, "Believe me, I would know."

"Who is in charge while he is away?"

"His steward."

Lord Tybalt smiled menacingly, "Change of plans."

Chapter 15

Peter matched Charlotte's step as they trudged through Black-fire Wood. The griffins: Luna, Argentum and Draco brought up the rear. As they continued their walk, Peter felt the urge to know what exactly Charlotte had in mind. "Charlotte, I'm afraid I don't know what the plan is. Do you even have one?"

"Of course," Charlotte answered, "I need to find that bird."

Peter gave her a puzzled expression, "Pardon?"

"That bird the legend speaks of," Charlotte replied. "I believe that it is the key to defeating Lord Tybalt."

"You mean to tell me that you want to find something that might not even exist. Charlotte, your kingdom is in peril, you must lean on something more reliable and realistic."

Charlotte stopped altogether and spun around to face Peter. Her green eyes blazed back at him as she spoke, "Peter, listen. I know what I'm doing. You don't need to worry about the kingdom, that's my role."

"My role includes making sure you, Charlotte, are safe as well as Aurum. It was the last order your father gave to me."

Charlotte cocked her head, "My father? What do you mean?" Before he could answer, she quickly asserted, "It doesn't matter. From now on, you listen and do as I say."

Peter gazed into her flaming eyes and nodded his consent. Nothing could change her mind.

After a few more long, tiring hours of walking, Charlotte stopped before a small field-like opening in the forest. "It's growing dark, we should stop for the night."

Peter observed his surroundings. The opening was covered with rich, green grass and bordered with mossy rocks. The large elm trees creaked as a soft breeze blew through the twilight sky. Charlotte rubbed her arms fervently and edged closer to Luna. Peter walked over to Draco and opened a burlap sack he had hastily strapped to the beast's back. Revealing a piece of flint and steel, he said, "I'll start up a fire. Who knows how cold it will get."

Charlotte nodded, "I'll fetch some wood."

After collecting a bundle of dried sticks, twigs, and a few logs, Peter knelt down and began to scrape the flint and steel together over a dirt patch he had cleared. Chipping off red-hot pieces of steel, Peter held a dry twig to the hot metal. The stick began to shrivel up and smolder, causing bright, red flecks to appear on the wood. Finally, after a few more tedious minutes, the hot steel caught fire on the twigs and began to ignite in flaming orange and yellow colors. Peter threw a larger piece of wood into the makeshift fireplace and sat back to watch the tongues of fire eat away at the dry log. Charlotte sat across from him, leaning against Luna while Argentum crouched nearby. Luna's feathery tail flicked back and forth across Charlotte's legs and her large cat-like body curled around Charlotte, creating a warm blanket from the dropping temperature. Draco lay beside Peter sleeping. Every now and then the beast would perk up to the sound of the fire crackling. Peter continued to watch the embers burn, wondering how Charlotte's kingdom could be in peril on such a peaceful night as this. He watched as the young queen nuzzled against Luna as a pillow and drifted off to sleep. Feeding another log to the hungry flames, Peter leaned against a mossy rock. Groaning, he struggled to get comfortable. Draco's head shot up again. This time, instead of laying back down, Draco stood up and walked over to Peter. The griffin let out a low guttural sound and moved between Peter and the boulder. Draco laid down once again and flicked his tail over Peter's waist. Peter leaned into the beast'e soft fur and fell into a deep sleep.

A low rumble caused Peter to jolt upright. Looking up, he noticed a sizable amount of clouds billowing their way across the gray sky. In a few minutes nature would be crying her rain upon the earth, showering the land in her tears. Peter glanced at Charlotte still sound asleep near Luna and Argentum. Draco got up from behind Peter and paced back and forth near the ashes of the fire pit. Standing, Peter stretched his drowsy muscles and looked towards the forest. While traveling yesterday, he had caught the sound of a stream. Perhaps if he was quick he would be able to wash his face and hands before the rain started.

His eyes fell back on Charlotte huddled next to Luna. He smiled at the timid look the young queen portrayed. No one would ever guess she was a strong and firm leader. Peter started to walk softly to her. The second he got too close to Luna's liking, the beast let out a growl. The griffin wrapped a protective tail over Charlotte's slim figure and continued with her deep growling. Peter put out a hand to the beast's beak, "Luna, it's me, Peter. Do not worry, I'm not here to harm her. Relax."

After a few seconds, the griffin's aggressiveness eased and Peter moved towards Charlotte once more. All the while holding his hand out to Luna, assuring her he meant no harm. He placed a hand on Charlotte's shoulder and rubbed it gently. "Charlotte…" he whispered.

Before he knew what happened, a pair of green eyes shot open and a dagger met his throat. Charlotte's cold, green gaze was as sharp as the blade that she pressed against his throat. "Charlotte," he repeated, forcing his voice to remain calm, "It's Peter, don't you recognize me?"

The dagger left his throat and returned to its sheath. "Peter, I'm sorry. It's an immediate reaction," Charlotte sighed. Rubbing her eyes, she peered at him like a sleepy child, "What is it?"

"I just wanted to alert you that I'm on my way to find that stream I heard yesterday. Would you like to come?"

Charlotte yawned and shook her head, sending waves of ebony hair cascading down her back, "No, you go. I'll stay here with the griffins."

Peter nodded, "Very well." He squeezed her hand, "I'll be back shortly."

She smiled, yawned once more, and fell back into Luna's sleek, black fur.

Peter jogged towards the shimmering body of water ahead of him. Scanning the rocky shore he took in the tranquil scene around him. The stream wound its way through the woods like a large, blue snake. Pebbles covered the shore and the occasional jagged rock split through the water's surface. Elms lined the shore front and shaded a good half of the water, creating a deep blue color. Lastly, a small waterfall pumped water into the stream from the upper stream above a wall of rocks. Gray clouds still stubbornly blotted out the sun. Peter knelt down and began to wash his hands. He'd better hurry if he didn't wish to be caught in the downpour.

After dowsing his face several times with the icy spring water, a flash of lightening illuminated the sky followed by a crackling sound of thunder. Looking towards the heavens, Peter saw another spark of lightening slice across the cloudy atmosphere. Hurriedly, he looked around for a suitable shelter from the storm. Peter's gaze caught sight of a small, dark cave sitting behind the small waterfall near the stream. Not the best shelter from a thunderstorm, but it would have to do. He rushed into the cave as another rumble of thunder shook the earth. He stood there in the dark, his thoughts wandering quickly back to Charlotte. Hopefully she was luckier than him in finding shelter. Perhaps a place that was dry. Peter looked down at his legs, knee deep in frigid spring water. He could feel the cold liquid filtering through his leather boots. Stifling a gasp of surprise, he looked around. He could see nothing but the gap to the stormy outside.

The wind picked up speed and howled, blowing rain into the cave, slapping drops in Peter's face. Annoyed, he backed further into the cave, sloshing through the freezing water. Feeling his hand against the cold, rough wall, he wondered just exactly how deep this cave went. His question was answered when his back smacked against a hard object. Groaning, he massaged his back and shoulders, it was a lot larger than he had expected. From the outside, the cave looked like it could hardly fit a person kneeling down, let alone one standing up.

A short rush of wind blew through Peter's brown hair, sending it into his eyes. Frowning, he raked it back forcibly. The wind couldn't possibly reach him from inside here. Or was it wind? He turned around and squinted through the blackness. No use, he couldn't see anything. He felt the wall in front of him. Instead of his fingers meeting solid rock, they met a feathery, soft object. Fiery heat started to seep into his fingers. Peter snatched his hand away from the heat source. Strange. Walls weren't soft and burning with heat. Was it a wall? Starting to feel uneasy, he started to back up towards the entrance. He would rather stand in rain than share shelter with a strange creature he couldn't see. Suddenly, an eagle's loud war cry split the air and shook the earth far worse than any thunder ever could.

———————

Charlotte shot up at the thundering furor that erupted somewhere within the forest. Looking out from her shelter in the trees, she gazed about for the cause of such a noise. It was coming from farther in. Her mind froze. From the exact same area Peter had told her he was going. Quickly, she unhitched the knapsack from Draco's back and bundled all of their supplies against a thick, elm trunk. She snapped Luna over and ordered the black griffin to stay. Out of all the griffins, Luna was the most protective and Charlotte knew she could trust the beast with their belongings. Snapping her fingers, Draco and Argentum came instantly to her side. Making sure her sword was strapped tightly, Charlotte leapt onto Argentum's back and let her and Draco take to the sky.

———————

Peter scampered clumsily through the dark. Turning up waves in the cold water as he ran headlong towards the cave entrance. Reaching the opening, blinding sunlight struck his dark-adjusted eyes. The eagle's piercing scream still rang fresh in his ears. Something was in that cave. He didn't know what, nor did he intend to stay and find out. He sloshed across the stream to the rocky bank, his clothes dripping with icy water. Shivering, Peter stumbled into the woods and collapsed against a tree.

A cry split the air, making him jump up and draw his sword. Instead of coming from the cave, it traveled across the land from the now clear sky up above. He watched as the two griffins, Argentum and Draco, landed beside the stream and a slim figure jumped to the ground. "Peter?" Charlotte's voice met his ears.

Sheathing his weapon and trying his best not to shiver, Peter made his way towards her. "I'm here," he called.

Charlotte's eyes widened in shock as she looked Peter up and down. "Whatever happened to you? I thought your plan was to wash up not drench yourself in cold, spring water."

For the first time in awhile, Peter caught Charlotte trying her best to hide a laugh. He could feel his cheeks start to burn in humiliation. He sure disliked being laughed at. "I can explain this," he said, gesturing to his drenched clothing.

She walked over to him, "Yes, you can. But first, Peter, we must get you back to camp and into some dry clothes, for you'll become ill if you stay in such attire."

Peter nodded his consent and looked back at the cave. He could still hear the piercing cry in his mind. He shivered. "Let's go, Charlotte. I'm afraid there's more to tell than it seems."

———————

After a change into dry clothing, Peter sat by a crackling fire, a wool blanket on his lap for extra warmth. With the peaceful atmosphere surrounding him, it was hard to believe the events of the morning had actually occurred. But as he looked down at his fingers and saw the burn mark surrounding his entire hand, he knew it was true. Peter watched as Charlotte added another log to the fire, sending orange sparks flying to the air and being carried off by the wind. A small metal pot lay above the fire propped up by sticks far enough away not to burn. The fragrance of sweet-smelling stew rising from the steam, met Peter's nose. He took a deep breath of the aroma and sighed, "How did you manage to cook up something out here?"

"Luna found some rabbit meat while you were away," she replied simply. "After she killed it, I cleaned it with my dagger and gathered other herbs and vegetation from around the forest. I'm accustomed to hunting and gathering my own food, for it's the way I was raised."

"I must say, I am impressed," Peter replied, watching Charlotte stir the stew once more. "You truly know how to do everything. Most queens would turn up their nose at such a distasteful job."

Charlotte smiled and sat down next to him. "As you can see, I'm not like most queens, or most women, in fact."

Her eyes turned to look into the distance, beyond the trees, "Not after all I've been through."

Peter felt the growing urge to ask her about her childhood again. He clasped her hand in his and began softly, "Charlotte, please, can you…"

"What happened to your hand?" she exclaimed suddenly, turning the conversation from herself.

Peter pulled his hand away, but Charlotte snatched it back and observed his bright, red mark. "Er…I burned it." He tried to pull it away again but she held it firmly, "Truthfully, it's nothing. I'm fine."

She glanced up at him, "I don't believe you." She smiled slightly and squeezed his hand.

He let out a gasp and yanked his hand away, "Whatever was that for?"

"To see if you were telling the truth or not. I can see that you're not, considering your reaction to my touch."

"You squeezed my hand," he retorted. "If you had simply left it alone it would have been fine."

Her face molded into concern. "I doubt that," she answered grimly, "I have had experience with burns before and I recognize agony when I see it."

He groaned, "Honest Charlotte, you needn't…"

"How did you manage to burn yourself?" she interrupted.

"In a cave," was all he answered.

Charlotte gave him a dubious look, "A cave?"

"Yes. I ran into a…well…I can't say for sure, but some kind of creature." He saw Charlotte's mouth open. He held up his hand, "Don't ask me what, for I don't know."

"Describe it then?" she demanded.

"I'm afraid I can't. I couldn't see."

"How did it feel?" she pressed.

"Rather soft and feathery, until it burned my hand." Peter replied, frowning down at his burned hand.

Charlotte nodded absently, "I think I might know what you ran into. But I would have to see it to be sure."

"What do you think it was?"

"I won't say a word about it until you take me there to see it."

Realizing where she was leading with the conversation, Peter jumped up and said fiercely, "Absolutely not! I will not put your life in danger."

Charlotte clucked her tongue and got up to stand beside him. "Peter, you do realize that I was very observant when I flew to the stream. I am quite capable of traveling there by myself. So," she continued, walking over to stew pot, "if you refuse to take me, I will simply go alone." She held up her hand when he began to protest, "And don't worry about my safety, for I shall be perfectly fine." With that, she began to dish out the stew.

Peter looked up into the sky and took a deep breath, letting it out slowly. Charlotte was right. He couldn't stop her from going and he knew she would leave without him. Pinching the bridge of his nose, Peter said reluctantly, "Fine, I will do as you wish. I can't stop you from going but I can protect you."

She stared at him through vexed eyes, "Nonsense, I can take care of myself." Then, her gaze softened and turned mischievous. Walking over to him, she handed him a bowl of stew, "Since you agreed to come along, you may have your supper."

"You mean to say that you wouldn't have given me anything if I had refused?" he asked incredulously.

She shrugged her shoulders and plopped down beside him with her own bowl, "Perhaps, perhaps not."

"Charlotte!" Instead of rage, he felt laughter bubbling in his throat from her cleverness. He let out a soft laugh and began to eat.

"Your hand doesn't pain you when you hold a bowl or spoon?" Charlotte asked.

"Charlotte, my hand is burned, not broken. I'm close to becoming a knight, I'm used to slight pains."

She shrugged once more and turned back to finishing her stew. "Tonight you can rub a lotion on it to sooth the pain and to prevent swelling."

Early the next morning, Peter and Charlotte rose and, after a quick breakfast of cold stew, began their preparations for the flight to the cave. It was decided that they would leave Draco with the supplies and take the other two griffins, Luna and Argentum. Peter strapped on his sword and added a small dagger to his belt for extra protection. He flexed his burned hand in irritation. The lotion he had put on last night had prevented some of the swelling and eased some of the pain, but now it was starting to come back. He considered asking Charlotte for some more of the pain-remover but shoved the idea aside. It wouldn't be very beneficial in the end, considering the burn was on his right hand, his sword hand. Aside from the burn, the lotion would only make it even more difficult to hold and wield his weapon.

"Are you ready?"

Peter looked to see Charlotte already mounted on Luna. Nodding, he swung up onto Argentum's back and the two set out for the cave.

Minutes later, they landed beside the stream and Peter swung down to observe the cave. The sound of pebbles crunching together told him Charlotte stood beside him. She nodded to the dark chamber, "This is the cave you spoke of?"

"Yes," was all he said, wondering what danger they would come upon when they entered.

"Well then, shall we go?" Taking care to order the griffins to remain where they were, Charlotte started forward, clutching the hilt of her sword.

Peter hurried ahead of her and stood in his tracks, "Hold a minute, Charlotte. I'm going in first just to make sure everything is...safe." Even as he said the word, Peter knew nothing was 'safe' about the cavern.

Charlotte let out a groan, "Peter, can you not see I can fend for myself? Besides, if anything goes amiss I shall have Luna and Argentum."

"I know, but please. I really don't want anything to happen to you."

She let out another frustrated groan but said, "Suit yourself, but it shall all be for not, for I intend to go in there whether you agree or disagree."

Peter ignored her comment, "Thank you." Holding up his hand he added firmly, "Wait here until I call for you."

Peter approached the cave cautiously and stared down at the cave's floor. Water. He would have to drench his clothing in cold spring water again. Taking a deep breath he plunged in. Biting back a cry, he felt the water seep into his clothing. Forcing to ignore the cold biting at his skin, he splashed through the waist deep water. The cave was brighter in full daylight with the sun. The only reason for it being dark last time was because of the storm. Now, he could make out the basic outline of the lair. The cave resembled an upside-down world. Plants, dirt, and moss clung to the ceiling, while the ground was full of deep blue water. Everything seemed to be fine. Peaceful. Nothing was here. As Peter started back to deliver the news to Charlotte, a snapping from up above made him freeze. Forcing his gaze back up to the ceiling, Peter's gaze settled on a giant, fiery red and orange bird. The bird stared at him through golden eyes and walked along its perch strung to the ceiling by thick vines. As quietly and quickly as possible, Peter drew his sword, ignoring the pain of his burn. Now he had found the source of his mark and of the uprising during the storm. Here sat a beast bigger than the griffins. Here was the creature that set fire to its feathers. Here was the mysterious legendary beast.

Chapter 16

Peter could feel his sword hand grow clammy as he watched the giant bird study him from head to toe. Peter remained frozen and searched his mind frantically for an idea. He was afraid that if he moved the beast would attack and if he called for help, the beast might attack as well. Plus, he wouldn't dare put Charlotte in such a dangerous position, not when he intended to protect her. His debate with himself would end when he decided on remaining still and waiting patiently for the giant bird to lose interest. Then, he would seize that moment to escape.

The large beast started to descend from its perch and come towards him. Still, Peter forced his limbs not to move. Any sudden movement could cause this creature to burst into an outrage of fury. The bird came down to ground level and, to Peter's surprise, began to swim towards him. Once the beast was close enough for Peter to reach out and touch it, his feet betrayed him. The single footstep back made the water seem to echo loudly across the walls. Silence enveloped the boy and beast. Peter stared into the piercing golden eyes, wondering what to make of the situation. Just as an escape plan began to form in his mind, the bird let out an ear-piercing screech. Peter ducked and swerved towards the right as the bird launched itself up into the air. The impact of the wings shoved Peter forward, sending him toppling into the water and losing his balance. The black water crowded around his body, forcing water in his eyes and nose. The dead weight of his sword lowered him further down, causing Peter's lung to scream for air. He released his sword and grabbed blindly for an object to hoist himself up. His fingers met only water. Forcing his rising panic down, Peter remained still and let himself float up. As soon as his head broke the water, Peter filled his hungry lungs with rich oxygen.

Another enraged scream hit the air and he caught sight of the giant bird swooping towards him. Now, without his sword, Peter groped desperately for his only other weapon, a dagger. Drawing the small blade, Peter braced himself in the choppy water. Just before smacking into him, the bird flew higher and seized Peter's right arm in its sharp talons and flew out of the cave. Letting out a cry of pain, Peter watched in horror as the bird's talons lit into flames. Searing pain vibrated through his shoulders and he let out another cry, louder than the other.

"Peter!"

He looked down to see Charlotte running frantically following the bird as the beast rose in the sky. Noticing the dagger still in his hand, Peter ignored the fiery pain that wreathed around his right shoulder and arm and struck at the bird's talons. The beast screamed in response and dropped him only to pick him from the sky again, this time by the tunic over his neck. The tunic pressed against his throat, choking him. Heat started to burn towards his neck and hair and Peter's heart began to pick up even more speed. If his neck and hair caught on fire...he refused to think further.

A flash of black and silver whipped past him and Peter noticed Luna and Argentum surrounding the giant bird and screaming their outrage. Craning his neck upward, Peter saw Argentum come up to the bird's stomach and ram her beak into its soft underside. The bird screamed in anger and flew closer to the ground, releasing Peter. Toppling through the air, Peter hit the ground with a hard thud, robbing him of his breath. He watched as Argentum and Luna beat the giant bird back into its lair. The sound of running feet and a soft voice calling his name echoed in Peter's ears as he fought against unconsciousness. After a few failed attempts to stay awake, Peter closed his eyes and the world around him went black.

Peter woke and let out a loud groan of pain as he noticed Charlotte washing his burned shoulder and arm gently with a cloth. Charlotte looked up at him, "You're awake."

Peter gave her a wry smile and nodded. When she turned to continue her washing, he edged away and looked at the cloth in uneasiness. She gave him a sympathetic smile, "I knows it pains you, Peter, but you must remain still. If I don't wash the burn it might get infected."

Peter shrugged and reluctantly let her continue, biting his lip to prevent himself from crying out as another jolt of searing pain shot through his arm. He squinted around at his surroundings and tried to figure out where he was. When he last was awake, he was dropped from the sky by the bird-like creature. Now, it was dark and he was back at camp watching a fire dance across the logs. Luna and Argentum lay beside each other sleeping. Seeing not a scratch on the two female griffins, Peter was relieved they had at least come out uninjured. Draco lay by the fire taking a cat-nap.

Peter fixed his eyes on Charlotte once again, ready to beg for her to stop and let his physician handle such a nasty burn. But as he observed her wash his wound with intent and concerned eyes, he stopped himself. Why not let her care for him for a time? She would definitely do a much better job than any physician he hired. He watched the firelight dance across her features and glisten into her pure, green eyes, alive with concern for him. Despite the searing pain, he smiled at her. This was the gentle, caring queen he had wished to see again ever since she had taken Gavin back home. Now, the same loving nature was displayed before him again. Charlotte stopped rinsing his shoulder and arm and set the cloth down. "Thank you," he managed to murmur.

"I'm not finished yet," she replied.

Peter watched as she pulled a bowl from behind her and spooned up a green paste. He edged away at the sight of the strange substance. "What on earth is that?" he asked.

"This paste decreases swelling and prevents infection," she informed him, scooting closer to take his arm gently. Peter winced as she applied the mixture. "I sure hope this substance serves its purpose," he said, through clenched teeth.

"Well, perhaps next time you will not concern yourself so much about keeping me safe," Charlotte said grimly.

Sudden remorse hit him. To think he mightn't be in such a state if he had let Charlotte help him. He had silenced her before she could utter a single thought on the matter. Peter knew how well Charlotte was with mystical creatures, perhaps she could have helped. Instead, he made everything worse and nearly killed himself in the process. Peter took Charlotte's hand in his left one and rubbed it gently, "Forgive me, Charlotte. I acted foolishly. I should never have done what I did earlier."

She ceased rubbing the mixture on his arm and looked him in the eyes. "You are forgiven. But please, Peter, don't put yourself in such a dangerous position again," she begged.

"It's my duty as a squire and future knight to protect you and the kingdom of Aurum."

Charlotte looked down at her hand, which he still held, and pulled away. "Don't concern yourself with such a shallow prestige."

"Whatever would be shallow about wanting you safe and secure?" he asked rather taken aback by her comment.

She looked away. "Simply because..." she trailed off and didn't answer. Peter felt the urge to push her and get an answer but he scolded himself on the matter and replied softly, "Never mind, don't answer the question." Reaching out, Peter gently rubbed her shoulder, wanting to reassure her that he meant what he said. But, as if bitten by a serpent, Charlotte jerked away. He dropped his hand in surprise, "What's wrong?"

Her expression became guarded again and Peter could sense her steeling her emotions. "Nothing, I'm simply sensitive to anyone's touch. Even if it is a friendly handshake or respectful kiss on the hand, my mind doesn't settle right. Such gestures were never given to me in the past." Seeming to realize she had said too much, Charlotte dropped the subject abruptly and walked over to a burlap sack, opened the hood, and revealed a role of white cloth. "I shall wrap this around your shoulder and arm, that way it will help lessen the chance of infection."

Peter only nodded. He wouldn't give up the previous conversation so easily. She seemed to want to tell him something but remained wary of him in the end. Once Charlotte settled herself by his side and began to wrap his arm, Peter opened the subject again, "Charlotte, could you please tell me more of your past? I assure you, you can tell me anything." She stopped wrapping and stared up at him. Her green eyes were a sea of colliding emotions. Each opposing forces battling the other for the victory.

––––––––––––

Charlotte turned her gaze from Peter's intense blue stare. Her conscience seemed to rip in two. One side wanted her to remain the independent, hard girl she had trained herself to be; to remain guarded and refuse his kind demeanor. The other half wanted to believe Peter; to confess everything that had happened in her past. She opened her mouth several times, faltering with her words. Finally, she was able to find her tongue and pronounce enough words to make her message clear. "There's nothing more to be told." With that, she focused on securing his bandage, wanting greatly to change the subject. "There, it is complete," she announced, hoping to draw him into more important matters, "Just take care not to…" her speech failed once more when a warm hand guided her chin back up to Peter's gaze.

"You're hiding something from me, are you not?" he asked. Before waiting for her answer he continued. "I know it is hard for you, for you're built like a stone fortress. But you must understand that you cannot avoid this conversation much longer, you must take down this barricade between us. Perhaps if you do, then I will be able to help you."

She let out a deep, wavering breath and nodded slowly. If Peter ever was to understand her she must tell him everything.

Taking her nod for a 'yes' Peter began, "Charlotte, what happened to make you hate nobility so? I cannot forget the threats you gave me when we first met."

This question was the one which still caused her pain. Even though now, half of the answer wasn't fully true. But, seeing how determined Peter was, she decided to tell him. "It all started when I still lived with Alice and her family. I was merely eleven when it happened. I've been cautious around nobles ever since, even though I am one myself."

"What happened?" Peter asked softly.

"Alice and I were on our way to the village market to pick up supplies. When we got there, the market was in flames. Everything around us was on fire. We ran home, hoping to find nothing amiss. But, we were wrong. Our own cottage was in flames as well. We were incased in a wall of fire. Alice's father and brother were running towards us. Alice's father ordered me and his children into the woods. Telling us to keep running and never turn back. I did as I was told. Not until I was safely in Vetitum Wood did I realize that neither Alice nor her brother were with me. I called to them over and over again, wanting to go look for them, but not daring to brave the run through the blazing furnace."

Charlotte paused and looked at Peter. Seeing that he was still listening, she continued, "After searching the village of ashes, I told myself they were dead and that I would never set foot in the village from then on." Charlotte watched as Peter's eyes clouded with sympathy. Frowning she added, "That is why I am so guarded and cautious with other nobles. The landlord of my village had ordered every house to be burned and destroyed."

Peter sighed and nodded, "That village used to belong to Lord Roger before he died. I could easily see why he would do such a thing. He only thought of his own personal gain, never about how it may affect others." Peter smiled, "But, it is a relief to know that the village is now mine. You know I would never do such a thing. I give you my word."

Charlotte managed a smile, "That is why I gave you that piece of land as part of your reward. I knew you didn't have the heart to destroy an entire village."

"Now, one more question," Peter said. "Why are you sensitive to touch?"

"That connects with the fire." Pulling up her sleeve, Charlotte revealed a long, white burn mark. "This is the reason why. I have an identical one on my back and another on my shoulder. I didn't escape untouched by the hungry flames."

Peter only nodded.

"So, whenever someone reaches to give me a friendly gesture, it reminds me of the fire in my childhood."

Peter looked at her with sincere blue eyes and said gently, "Charlotte, you must realize I mean you no harm when I do so. I would never dream of hurting you."

———

Peter saw a new kind of light filter into Charlotte's eyes. It seemed like she wanted to accept the truth, to believe him. He allowed her to let his words sink in. Hopefully from now on she would open up to him and tell him all her troubles and worries. After another minute of peaceful silence, Charlotte spoke up, "You must get some rest. You're not fully yourself yet."

"I'm fine," Peter responded. "The only problem left is my shoulder and arm."

"Well then, I must get some sleep, for I have a very eventful morning ahead of me."

"You mean to say we do?" Peter corrected.

"No," she said firmly, "I do. You are going to rest off the morning while I track down that bird."

Shock pulsed through Peter as her last words echoed through his mind. Despite his pain, Peter jumped up next to her. "What on earth would possess you to go after that wretched beast?"

"It is not a 'wretched beast' as you put it," Charlotte retorted. "It is a phoenix. That is what the legend is speaking of."

"That doesn't mean you have to capture that... phoenix. Did you not hear what fate beheld those two hunters?"

"Peter, please," Charlotte implored. "Can you not trust me in this? I assure you, I will be fine!"

Peter let out an inward groan and pinched the bridge of his nose. Looking down at her beseeching stare, he reached out with his left hand to stroke her cheek. She jolted under his touch. "Be still, Charlotte," Peter said gently, "I shan't hurt you." She relaxed under his touch, making him feel strangely warm. "I simply don't want anything to happen to you," he said, continuing to stroke her soft cheek. "Give me a promise, Charlotte, that you will remain safe and do what is best for your kingdom."

"Yes, I give you my word," she responded. Pulling away from his hand, she ordered firmly, "Now, Peter, rest, for you won't gain strength without sleep."

"Very well," Peter sighed, "I will do as you say."

Lying on his left side, Peter winced as he made a sudden movement with his right shoulder. Closing his eyes, he succumbed to a restful sleep.

———————

Peter awoke to the flapping of large wings and screeches of surprise from the griffins. Sitting up, he rubbed his eyes to make sure he saw everything correctly. Sure enough, he did. Charlotte stood before him, flanked on either side by Luna and Argentum. Draco lay next to Peter, hissing. Behind Charlotte stood the massive phoenix. He jumped up in surprise, shock running through his mind. His gaze traveled from the phoenix to Charlotte for an explanation. "Charlotte, what is the meaning of this?"

Charlotte gave him a puzzled expression, "Whatever do you mean, Peter? I told you I would search out this phoenix. You shouldn't act so surprised."

Peter walked towards Charlotte and rose to his full height, now seeming to tower over Charlotte. "I thought we had agreed that you would remain safe and do what is best for your kingdom."

"We did. That is exactly why I went." Charlotte turned around to face the phoenix. Reaching up, she placed her hand on the large beast's beak. "My kingdom will only be secure if this giant fights on our side."

Peter ran a hand through his hair. "Very well." He couldn't argue with her. That never turned out well in the end. "What do you wish to do now?"

"I must return home and prepare for battle."

"As you wish," Peter replied. Peter walked back over to where Draco lay and placed a hand on the griffin's flank. Strapping his burlap sacks to Draco's back, Peter turned back to Charlotte. "Do you wish for me to escort you back to your fortress?"

"There is no need for that. Remember that you have been in the countryside."

Peter bowed his head, "Of course." He most certainly couldn't forget that detail.

After seeing that everything was packed safely away and strapped to the griffin's backs, the two were ready to go. It was decided that the phoenix would return with Charlotte to her castle where she would store it away until the bird was needed. Hoisting himself onto Draco's back, Peter turned to see Charlotte do the same.

"Peter?"

"Yes, Charlotte?"

"Thank you for your assistance. Your loyalty never wavers."

Peter smiled and nodded, "It is my pleasure and, of course, my duty."

She flashed him a smile, then turned serious, "Once I return I plan to send out messages to the lords of the council. From there, we will plan our battle."

"How do you suppose you shall lead the attack?" Peter asked. Lord Tybalt hadn't made any direct assaults and there was still no guarantee he was at the fortress in Malum Wood.

"Save your questions for the council," Charlotte answered. "I will alert you when it is time to plan, but for now I only wish to return home."

Chapter 17

Rowan paced to and fro, ringing his hands together as he nervously waited for Lord Peter to return from the countryside. He struggled to remain calm, but failed miserably when he thought of the horrible news he must break to his landlord. The whole bailey seemed to be waiting for the young noble. There was no usual bustle of activity. The orders were being fulfilled with silence and anxiety. Even the animals seemed to sense the change in the atmosphere and remained still. A griffin's screech was heard from the stables, causing Rowan to veer in that direction.

Lord Peter was striding towards him accompanied by a stable boy carrying his baggage. Rowan swallowed hard and went over his conversation once more like he had done so many times before. Only this time it was for real. He would break the news to the actual Lord Peter, the feudal overlord of Rowan's life. Lord Peter greeted him cheerfully, "Rowan! Whatever are you here for? Never mind," his landlord said when Rowan attempted to answer. Holding up his hand, Lord Peter continued, "Your timing is convenient for I…" the young noble trailed off and looked around the bailey. Rowan watched his landlord frown and speak up loudly, "Why is everyone so idle?"

At once, the servants quit eavesdropping and busily continued their jobs. But even as they worked, Lord Peter must have noticed the change of atmosphere, for his next words were, "What is the matter with everyone? I noticed a similar behavior in the stable boys."

Rowan folded his hands and forced himself to look Lord Peter straight in the eye. "My lord, may we speak alone?"

"Of course," Lord Peter replied. Frowning again he asked, "Where is Godfrey, he usually greets me?"

Rowan lowered his gaze, "You shall see in a moment." Rowan steered the young lord towards the Keep, "Come."

Once they entered the safety of Lord Peter's solar, the noble spun around, "Enough, Rowan. Tell me, what is the trouble?"

Rowan folded his hands together, this was going to be hard for Lord Peter to hear. He decided to start off slowly and proceed from there. Rowan met his lord's expecting gaze and began, "Your lordship has had nothing unusual since you left. Everything is normal."

Lord Peter didn't seem convinced. "Then why are my servants acting this way?"

"It's your steward Godfrey," Rowan replied.

"What of him? Speaking of which, were is my steward?" Peter asked, looking towards the door. "You said I shall see."

Rowan took a deep breath and began, choosing his words carefully. "Godfrey has left, my lord. He's gone."

Lord Peter stared at him blankly.

"There is no way to break this news to you gently."

"What? Explain, now!" Lord Peter demanded.

Rowan stared back at him, figuring out how to word his news.

"Rowan answer me! That's an order!"

Rowan jumped as the command rang out around the solar. He had never seen Lord Peter this angry before. The young noble's eyes flashed like blue tongues of fire. Normally, Lord Peter was a pleasant, slow to anger noble. Such fury startled Rowan. "Calm yourself, my lord. I will explain, but you must remain calm."

Lord Peter pinched the bridge of his nose, an act he always preformed when settling his temperament. "Very well, go on. I can manage."

"A day ago, Godfrey was given a sample of your lordship's wine. The servant said it was a new wine and wanted Godfrey's approval. Godfrey sampled the wine. Suddenly his features froze and he grabbed at his throat. Just before he collapsed, he murmured one word, "No." After that, Godfrey collapsed dead. Poisoned by the wine." Rowan stopped to let the startling news sink in.

Lord Peter only stared at him. His eyes clouding with a mixture of surprise and horror. Seeing his lordship's reaction made Rowan feel sick. He dared not imagine what this might do to the young lord. From what Rowan had heard, Godfrey was a steward to Lord Robert, Lord Peter's father. The steward was ever faithful and loyal in his work for Lord Peter's family and the noble seemed to have a close friendship with the steward. "I offer my condolences, great lord. A servant was sent to my cottage as soon as the death was proved. It was nightshade, a large dose of it as well. The servant said you, my lord, would take the news easier if I delivered it to you."

Lord Peter only nodded absently and stared through Rowan, dazed.

"Remember, my lord, I am here to offer my servitude. If you need my assistance I would be honored to serve you yet again."

Lord Peter only offered another halfhearted nod and turned towards his hearth. Walking over to a chair, the torn lord slumped into the furniture and stared into the dead ashes. Propping his elbows on his knees and burying his face in his hands he gave a muffled order, "Leave me."

Rowan bowed, "Of course." Backing out of the large solar, he shuffled silently down the Keep's stairs, leaving the young lord to grieve alone.

Peter stared absentmindedly out the solar's narrow window. The startling news rang fresh in his ears. His steward. The loyal and faithful Godfrey. Dead. Gone from Peter's life. Much like the grief that overtook him during his father's death. Peter didn't know how to react. Much to his discomfort, death was not an unusual occurrence in his life. It surrounded Peter in many ways. Battles, disease, weakness, childbirth, the list was endless.

He had already lost two influential people in his life, Lord Robert and King Philip. Now, his last close connection to his father, Godfrey, was gone. Peter couldn't help but feel downhearted. When Peter had been given his position three years ago, Godfrey had remained patient with him and informed him on easier ways to accomplish his new barony. If something went amiss, Godfrey got right to the bottom of the problem. Now he was gone. Never to be brought back. Two stray tears ran down his cheeks. He swiped at them angrily. He had no time for crying, especially now that he was older. Peter turned to the positive side of his life. There was one thing he could be thankful for. He had Rowan.

While Peter mourned, Rowan carried on being an excellent servant. Godfrey had taught the younger man well. Now, the old steward's teaching was coming to great use. Rowan was working non-stop, filling in Godfrey's old roles as best he could. He was quick to carry out Peter's every wish. The man fit naturally into the system.

According to his father's rules, Peter was supposed to hand over Godfrey's position to his bailiff, Bryce. But now, seeing Rowan getting along so well, Peter couldn't quite place Bryce in his new position. Bryce was Lord Robert's bailiff, but Peter had never really spoken to the man. Whenever Peter needed the bailiff to follow an order it was Godfrey who told Bryce. But perhaps he wasn't thinking correctly? The steward's sudden death still confused him. Perhaps confusion muddled his thinking? When his mind cleared he would be able to think logically.

"My lord?"

Peter spun around to see Rowan standing by the door.

"Yes, Rowan, come in," Peter began, "What is it?"

"A message came for your lordship. From the queen." Rowan handed Peter a creamy white envelope with Charlotte's emblem sealed on the back. Peter nodded and returned his gaze to Rowan. "Rowan, what is being done to justify my steward's death?"

"I have sent your best investigators on seeking out the murderer," Rowan answered, "Hopefully we shall soon have an answer."

Peter nodded once again, "Good, I'm relieved to hear something is being done about Godfrey's death. He was my last true connection to my father." Sadness overwhelmed him again and he looked down. Only then did he remember the letter he still held. Peter tore off the seal, opened the letter, and began to read:

My loyal and faithful subject Lord Peter,

"I request your presence today at high noon in order to discuss my upcoming battle plans. Please make hast, for I cannot proceed without your judgement."

Queen Charlotte of Aurum

Peter folded up the letter and turned his attention back to Rowan. "Inform a stable boy to ready my horse."

"Lord Peter, thank you for joining us so quickly," Charlotte's voice echoed across the Great Hall.

"Of course, my great queen." Peter took his place beside Lord Geoffrey and Lord Edmund. Every council member seemed to be there except for Lord Morris. Even if the young noble was a bit of an annoying coxcomb, his absence was disturbing. Must they lose yet another council lord. Ever since the death of Morris' father, Lord Francis, Lord Roger, and Lord Robert, the council's numbers were dwindling. Thankfully Charlotte had considered adding a few more men to her meeting. Peter's instructor, Sir Randolph, Sir Richard, and lastly Sir Henry. Some of the best military strategists in the kingdom.

"We are ready to proceed," Charlotte announced from her throne. "As you lords know, I have recently returned from my trip. In my time there, I have come to the conclusion that I have everything necessary to begin an attack on Lord Tybalt's fort." Her gaze turned to Sir Randolph, "Sir Randolph, you along with the Lord Peter, Sir Richard and Sir Henry were the ones who aided me in my escape. Did you successfully scout the area?"

"Lord Peter was the only one to fully take in the surroundings," Sir Randolph said, gesturing in Peter's direction. "He can inform you of the fortress' security."

All attention flicked to Peter. "Lord Peter?" Charlotte asked.

"The garrison is heavily guarded," Peter began, "and I expect we shall never again have the element of surprise near the sally port. Lord Tybalt has probably doubled security around that area."

He looked into Charlotte's eyes and saw a flicker of dismay enter, then retreat. She frowned, "Is that all, Lord Peter?"

"I did notice, however, that the fortress' walls are weak from old age. Evidently that stronghold has been there for generations. If we had a few battering rams we could easily crumble the walls."

Charlotte nodded, "If it is what you say, we could lay siege to the fortress and destroy Lord Tybalt's only defense. He'll have nowhere else to run."

"It is possible," Sir Richard replied. "The only alarming reason would be that of weapons."

"Sir Richard speaks the truth, my queen," Sir Henry jumped in, "Siege weaponry is a costly lot and takes rather long to build."

"How many weapons do you estimate it will take, Lord Peter?" Charlotte asked, turning to him once again.

Peter quickly envisioned Lord Tybalt's fortress. Calculating a quick estimate he replied, "From what I recall, I would say four to five weapons per side. If you wish to use such weapons, the greatest amount would be twenty."

"In which case, my queen," Sir Henry butted in, "that amount of siege weapons would take months to build."

Charlotte's disappointment only lasted a few seconds before it was replaced with a sudden realization. "Do you have any trebuchets or mangonels, Sir Henry?"

Sir Henry frowned as if trying to remember, "Only one trebuchet. I'm afraid that doesn't do much, your highness."

"It might," Charlotte replied. She turned her attention to Sir Richard, "What of you, Sir Richard?"

"I have one battering ram and a trebuchet that's nearly built," the knight answered.

Charlotte went around to each knight and noble and had them give their weapons report. Finally Peter's turn came. He cleared his throat and informed, "I'm afraid I don't have much, my queen. I have only a couple of ballistas and one battering ram. With all our siege weapons combined it amounts to only half of what we need."

"Everything counts," Charlotte advised. "I will tell my bailiff to double the speed the blacksmiths and carpenters are working on just now. I expect you all to do the same, my lords."

"But, my queen," Lord Edmund protested, "Perhaps we should besiege Lord Tybalt's fortress before. That way we could starve him and his followers out."

Charlotte considered the plan. After some contemplation the young queen answered, "I suppose we could try. In a way it could help lay siege to his stronghold. We could weaken them with hunger first."

"What if the plan doesn't work?" Lord Geoffrey asked with worry.

Charlotte leaned forward and looked Lord Geoffrey squarely in the eyes, "It will work."

Chapter 18

Peter sat behind his desk, his elbows propped up in front of him, watching the white tent flaps blowing gently in the breeze. He leaned his chin on his palm and contemplated Charlotte's battle plan. In order to avoid detection, Charlotte had set up their camp outside of Malum Wood and in the lush protection of Black-fire Wood. Early tomorrow morning they would trek the last remaining distance and besiege Lord Tybalt's fortress. Only if there were no more options, would Charlotte lay full siege to the enemy's stronghold. The queen's plan was to starve Lord Tybalt and his forces into surrender. Even with Charlotte's confidence, Peter's mind was beginning to fill with second thoughts and worry. There was a chance that Lord Tybalt would remain unyielding and refuse to surrender even if he had to watch each of his men die before him. If such a thing were to happen, Charlotte would lead an assault. If she had to follow up on such a plan there was a high chance of failure. They didn't possess half the weapons they needed. Their men in arms was large for the most part. But there was no telling how many men Lord Tybalt had since Peter and the other knights had rescued Charlotte.

Peter let his head slide to the desk before him. He needed some strong reassurance and wisdom from someone who was more experienced in the matter. Before death had claimed him, it had been King Philip. Then, it had been Godfrey. His steward would surely offer him some advice. Another unexpected wave of grief crashed over his thoughts. With all the preparations of war and battles, Peter had had no time to think of his old steward. But now alone with his troubled thoughts he had plenty of time. Before he could succumb to another distant grief-stricken world, Rowan peeked in from outside, "My lord?"

Peter quickly shoved his grief down for another time, "Yes, Rowan?"

"Her Majesty, the queen, wishes to speak with you," Rowan informed.

Peter got up. His thoughts could wait. Right now, he had his duties to fulfill. "Very well. You may take me to the queen."

Peter followed Rowan through the small battle camp and took in his surroundings. War horses and coursers grazed nearby, squires sharpened and shined their knights' armors and blades, huge mangonels and trebuchets lay surrounding the ring of snow-colored tents, and many knights and lords gathered in groups to discuss the upcoming battle. A large, velvet tent loomed ahead of Peter, bearing the royal emblem of a golden griffin on its flagpole. A maidservant stood outside, hands folded in front of her. Rowan spoke a few words to the girl before she departed into the dark tent ahead. After a few seconds, the maid returned and walked over to Peter. Curtsying deeply she said, "Her Majesty is waiting, my lord."

Peter nodded and followed the maidservant inside the tent. Once his eyes adjusted to the dimness, he took note of Charlotte's pacing form. Her hands were drawn close together in front of her and she rang them vigorously. Peter had come to relate the action to stress. The maid scurried silently near Charlotte to alert her of her company, and Charlotte perked at the change in her environment and turned towards him. She fixed him with a gaze of vibrant green that stood out among the tent's velvet drapes.

He bowed formally and said, "Your Majesty, you summoned me. Is something disturbing you?"

"Why must something be disturbing me when I send for you?" she questioned. "You must accept, Lord Peter, that I do not only send for you in my need."

"Of course, my queen. I understand." Peter remained bowed waiting for his permission to stand.

"You may rise," Charlotte announced.

Peter obeyed. "What is it you wish, my queen?"

"You must accompany me for a stroll through the woods."

Peter was taken aback from her matter-of-fact tone and strange request. "I, my queen?" Peter asked, making sure he had heard correctly.

"Yes." Charlotte shot her maid a glare as if it were the girl's fault. "Some do not find it suitable that I travel alone. They fear something will happen to me."

Peter had to agree with whomever Charlotte was referring to. They were too close to enemy territory for her to wander about. If someone was needed to accompany her for protection, he was glad he was chosen. Nothing would happen to her under his watch. "As you wish, my queen."

———————

"Lord Cromwell!" Lord Tybalt's voice rang out with rage.

Lord Cromwell strode towards the lord's chair in the dark room. "Yes, my lord?"

"I have just heard from some of my scouts that the queen has set up an army camp nearby. Explain yourself!"

Lord Cromwell fell into utter confusion. Was he supposed to share some responsibility in the matter? He stammered out his answer, "I assure you, my lord, I had no idea the queen would have the gall to..."

"Shut up!" Lord Tybalt snapped back in fiery fury. "Enough jouncing around the matter. Go assess the current situation yourself. Lead a raid on the queen's camp tonight. I shall finish them off once and for all!"

"Of course, Lord Tybalt. Whatever you think necessary."

"Where's that blasted boy you keep with you?" Lord Tybalt demanded.

"He's in his room," Lord Cromwell informed.

"Take him with you. It's high time the boy earned his keep! So far he's been nothing but a bother!"

"Yes, my lord."

"Take the forest route." Lord Tybalt leaned forward in his chair and, with each word dripping like toxic poison, he ordered, "And if it's no trouble, kill everyone in your path."

———————

A steady breeze surrounded Charlotte as she strolled side by side with Peter in the lush, green forest. Her heart warmed with the familiar comfort of nature around her. The forest had been her source of refuge since she was a child. Whenever stress overtook her, she fled to the forest's comforting presence. The only thing she wished for most was to be alone with her thoughts during such times. But, despite her constant reassurance that she could fend for herself, her maid insisted she bring along a bodyguard. Rather than have a stranger walk with her, Charlotte had requested Peter's presence. Charlotte was starting to realize that Peter could be a second choice of refuge in the future. Thinking of him now, she couldn't help but note how quiet and reserved he seemed. She had never seen these characteristics in him before. Normally by this time he would have started a conversation. "What is troubling you, Peter? You're unusually quiet."

"Nothing." Was his only reply.

Charlotte knew his answer was pointless. His voice and demeanor had easily betrayed him. "There must be something. You are never so reserved with me. Tell me, I beg you."

His voice sounded distant as he replied, "My steward, Godfrey, was murdered not long ago."

Shock overtook Charlotte. Murdered? Godfrey? Who would commit such an audacious crime? "I offer my deep condolences, Peter," she replied as softly as possible. She was rather inept in such areas as sympathy.

"I'm improving," he said. "I only grieve slightly now, for the upcoming siege has left me busy."

Charlotte knew it was unhealthy for him to keep such experiences hidden. She had done it with her own family and suffered dreadfully from it. If Peter were to succumb to grief, he would become like her and she would hate to see him so cold and hard. "How did it happen?" Charlotte asked in a whisper.

"He was poisoned," Peter answered bitterly.

"Poisoned?"

"Someone put nightshade in my wine. Godfrey was asked to sample it. He died shortly afterward." Peter grew quiet and continued to walk with Charlotte in silence.

"He died nobly," Charlotte said after a few minutes of silence.

Peter shook his head in disbelief and confusion, "How, Charlotte? There is nothing noble about dying from nightshade poison."

"He died to save your life. He favored you so greatly that he was willing to face death for your life," Charlotte explained, gentleness forming every word. "One code of the knights is to fight for and protect the innocent. You were innocent of whatever someone held against you. Godfrey knew this, Peter. He protected you, the innocent, with his life."

Peter stopped walking to turn and look down at her. "How do you know all of this, Charlotte? How can you say such things to me and make me feel better?"

"Because I've seen what grief does to people who don't allow themselves to grieve in a healthy way," she answered. "I'm one of those people and look how it affected me. I do not wish to see you so cold and heartless. I needed to reassure you that Godfrey's sudden death was not in vain."

Peter smiled, "Then I thank you, Charlotte. You know the very things to say to me whenever I'm in such situations."

Charlotte bowed her head, "You've done much for me. I'm simply returning the favor."

———————

Peter tilted Charlotte's chin up to look into her eyes. Her gaze was one of pleasure and gentleness. Her speech was full of reassurance and confidence. After he had allowed her gentle voice to sooth his grief-stricken mind, he didn't feel as guilty for his steward's death. If Charlotte believed Godfrey would be willing to face death for him, then it meant he could.

A sudden rustling by the trail caught both their attention. Charlotte immediately jolted away from him and stiffened and Peter could imagine a layer of steel cover her eyes. Reacting with instinct, Peter took hold of his sword's hilt. He scoured the bushes along with Charlotte, trying to find the source of the noise. Judging by the noise's depth and sound, it was no small and harmless woodland creature.

"Who's there?" Peter asked, his voice raised in volume and his hand tightening on his sword hilt. "Show yourself."

Suddenly, Peter felt like he was seeing ghosts. The two figures that emerged from the undergrowth made him jolt in alarm. Before him stood the last two people he had expected to see. Morris and Simon; both had their swords drawn. Charlotte looked equally startled. The way Morris glared at Peter with such aggression made him feel uneasy. The older squire had had a dislike for him since he became a lord. Peter flicked his gaze to Simon. The younger boy didn't seem to enjoy this situation, but he possessed a look of determination in his eyes.

"Lord Morris, Simon," Peter began cautiously, "I didn't expect to see you here. I thought...we thought..."

"You thought what, Lord Peter?" Morris sneered back. "You thought I was dead. Well, it will take more than an ambitious feudal lord to kill me. I have unfinished business regarding you."

Peter looked at him in astonishment, "What are you speaking of, Lord Morris? I..."

"My name isn't Lord Morris anymore. It's Lord Cromwell. Lord Morris is dead."

The name struck a realization in Peter's mind. Rowan had said something of the sort. He had told Peter that he had spied on the account of a Lord Cromwell. Back then, Peter had no memory of a lord by that name. Now, it seemed to be Morris. "I don't...I don't understand."

"Of course you don't," Morris interrupted again. "You assume like everyone else that Simon and I died in the hands of the enemy."

"No, we assumed you were captured and held hostage," Peter clarified.

"Well you assumed wrong anyway," Morris countered. "I, along with Simon, are friends with Lord Tybalt. He has arranged a far richer reward for our services than Her Majesty ever supplied. We side with him now."

"That is treason to the throne of Queen Charlotte," Peter said in outrage.

"Oh, in the end it will be worth it. When you are deep in your grave, Lord Peter, you will wish you had protected the queen more."Morris' gaze traveled to Charlotte with a dangerous glint.

Instinct overtook Peter. He drew his sword. "You won't dare harm our queen. You'll have me to get through first."

"That's what I thought you would say, Lord Peter," Morris growled. "You assume the queen is yours to keep."

Peter heard a sword draw and the flashing of steel as Charlotte's sword flew into her hand. "I am no man's to keep," she hissed in aggression. "I will kill you if you even try to come near me," she threatened.

Peter knew by her tone Charlotte wasn't jesting. She was serious and would follow through with her threat with no hesitation.

Morris only chuckled, "We shall see, my beauteous queen."

Peter took a step forward, "What do you want the queen for? You've always despised me, not Her Majesty."

"Oh, that," Morris began, running his finger along his blade, "Let me just say it's your payment for ruining my life and plans."

"Morris, I don't understand. I have never ruined any of your plans and certainly not your life. You make no sense."

"You've ruined my life, only you don't see it as I do," Morris answered savagely. "I'm two years older than you and should rightfully have become knight and lord before you. But no, that didn't happen. Your father died leaving his whole barony for you to govern. The only reason I became a lord was because my father died in the battle against Morgana. I was overcome by jealously and pain as I watched the other squires, Richard and Henry, become knights before me. But most of all I watched the admiration from the other lords towards you. Like your father, you are well respected in the council, even though you're much younger. I decided then that I would make your life miserable. After the death of your father and King Philip, I thought that pain would suffice and show you how much pain I had gone through.

"But no, of course it didn't," Morris thrashed his sword towards Peter in disgust "You remained positive and rose even higher in favor with the other nobles and the queen. While I remained on the sidelines. So I did the last thing I thought might bring you down permanently. I sent a servant to kill Godfrey, your last connection to your father."

Peter stood frozen in place, not knowing what to make of Morris' plots.

"But instead of bringing you down from your high perch," Morris continued, "It brought you into closer favor with the queen. If there's one thing I still won't allow it's you achieving the rank of king."

"I have no intention of making him king," Charlotte growled, "No man shall be king in my realm."

Morris smiled evilly, "If you want to live, my pretty queen, you will hand over your throne to Lord Tybalt and come with me."

Peter advanced further towards Morris, "If I have to threaten you with death, I will. You will not harm her."

Charlotte started to walk over to Peter. Only to be blocked by Simon's blade.

"Simon!" Peter ordered, "step away and don't go near her. I'm astonished at you! What would posses you to turn against the kingdom? You have nothing against me or our queen."

I...well..." Simon began to stammer out an answer.

"Silence, boy!" Morris cut him off. "Finish her. If she doesn't hand over Aurum willingly, I'll beat her into submission at Lord Tybalt's fortress."

"Lord Cromwell," Simon protested. "This wasn't part of the plan. We only..."

"Plans change! Now do as I say!"

Peter had tolerated enough. His fellow squire no longer existed. He had killed himself one day in jealousy. The one who stood before Peter was a threat and an enemy to Charlotte. Before Lord Cromwell could react, he struck a blow with his sword at his adversary's stomach. Lord Cromwell blocked and struck back. Peter sidestepped and spun around to face Lord Cromwell's back, allowing him to get a full view of the situation. Charlotte was locked in a vicious combat with Simon, while he was dueling with Lord Cromwell. Peter struck out at Lord Cromwell, causing the noble to retreat. Gritting, Lord Cromwell regained his footing and swung at Peter, hard. "I won't let you win. I've lost too much already."

Peter blocked the blow and felt the force of the blade vibrate through his body. "You're threatening someone I must protect, you will not defeat me easily."

"But I will," Lord Cromwell replied as he bypassed Peter's swift blow. Lord Cromwell speared at Peter's stomach. "And I'll leave you here to bleed to death."

A sudden surge of fear filled Peter. It wasn't the usual battle fear he endured before a battle. It was a life-threatening fear. He had never considered his life in danger when he combated with other knights. But, they had not wanted him entirely dead. They only wanted to win and to do so they were forced to injure him. But Peter had always found a way to ward off their blows. Lord Cromwell wanted to kill him out of pure hatred. The noble also had a fair chance, for Peter's wounds from the phoenix hadn't entirely healed. But there was no alternative, Peter must fight or risk losing his life, but more importantly risk losing Charlotte.

Lord Cromwell maneuvered to Peter's left and swung at his unprotected neck. Peter ducked and brought his sword up and underneath his adversary's. Staggering backwards Lord Cromwell quickly regained ground and swung towards Peter once again. Peter swerved, ducked, and warded off Lord Cromwell's blows.

Out of nowhere fiery pain shot up his left arm. He pulled away with a groan and realized his arm was slit. The cloth of his doublet was sliced and revealed a long, ugly, wound. The wound stung as it began to ooze out Peter's blood. Lord Cromwell let out a snicker. Peter stepped back in order to prepare for more heavy blows. He'd have to tend to his injury later on. Lord Cromwell paced and seethed, glaring at Peter with a look of hatred and jealousy. If there was one thing Peter had learned about Lord Cromwell in this short time, it was this. The man was full of anger and hatred. One spark to those two things could have him fighting with blind eyes. Anger always seemed to blind a fighter's view.

He heard a shriek come from behind. Making sure to keep a close eye on Lord Cromwell, he turned his attention to the cry. To his horror, Charlotte lay upon the ground with Simon looming over her. Instead of delivering the final blow, Simon stepped back and flung his sword away. Falling to his knees, he exclaimed, "Forgive me, Your Majesty. I didn't mean to...I only was..."

"Simon!" Lord Cromwell demanded. "Knock her unconscious! It's high time you proved yourself useful!"

Simon stood and faced the angry overlord. "No, Lord Cromwell. You have already pushed me to my limits. I will not commit treason."

In rage, Lord Cromwell charged straight at Charlotte. Peter blocked his way and swung his sword at Lord Cromwell's head. The noble ducked and Peter felt something rock hard hit his head, leaving his world in darkness.

Charlotte watched as her friend collapsed in front of her and her enemy charge towards her, evil glinting in his eyes. On her fall, her sword had clattered out of her reach. She couldn't retrieve it because of her cut leg. She couldn't stand because of the constant pain. The throbbing in her leg continued as she lifted her weight. "You are strong like steel," her mind whispered to her. Charlotte gripped her concealed dagger. "You are queen. You are protector over your kingdom."

When her adversary reached her, he lifted his blade skyward, ready to knock her unconscious. A boy younger than her forced himself between her and the enemy. Charlotte's enemy knocked the boy aside carelessly and swung his blade high in the sky. Before he lowered it, Charlotte stood on her good leg. Quick as lightening her dagger was in her hand. Instinct took over and she drove the blade deep into her adversary's stomach.

Chapter 19

2 weeks later

Charlotte paced in the dark interior of her large tent. In the darkness of Malum Wood, she began to go over all that had transpired during the past couple of weeks. After Peter and she had returned to camp with Lord Cromwell's body and Simon as prisoner, she had immediately taken action and moved into besieging Lord Tybalt's fortress that day.

Now, two weeks later, there was still no sign of victory. Each day she'd awakened with a hope that the day for victory was near. Presently, as she paced through her candle-lit tent, her hope began to die. Today would be a day like the previous ones. The guards and men at arms would watch and wait for signs of surrender and today would divulge the same report as yesterday. Charlotte wished she would see a white flag soon, because if not, she would have to order an assault.

"My queen?" a voice sounded from outside.

"Yes, Sir Richard?"

"We brought you the prisoner," the knight's answer came.

"Bring him in," she ordered. Charlotte spun to face her maid, Amity, "Pull the tent flaps up and secure them in place, for I am ready to conduct a meeting."

"Yes, your highness," Amity replied.

Today, Charlotte had called for a meeting concerning what to do with her prisoner, Simon. He had remained under watch ever since that day in the woods. Now, after thinking it over, Charlotte would hear out her prisoner and decide his fate.

The tent flaps were drawn up but provided no light. The constant dark atmosphere contributed to the heavy evil presence Charlotte felt down to her bones. Flaps drawn, Sir Richard shoved Simon into the undercover. Sir Richard was followed by Sir Henry, Sir Randolph and the lords, Edmund, Geoffrey and Peter. Despite the darkness, Charlotte could see the disappointment shining in Peter's eyes. She knew how Peter must hate to see his fellow squire go through such treatment. But she had no choice. Simon had chosen his path and now he must pay for it. He was a threat to her kingdom and must be done away with.

Simon looked at her, fear reflecting in his eyes. Charlotte frowned and stared back at him with cold eyes. She knew what she must do. Sympathy would never be shown to her enemy. Simon knelt down before her with his head hung in guilt.

"Squire Simon," she began icily, "you are guilty of treason to the throne and the kingdom of Aurum. What say you for yourself?"

"I had no intention to hurt you, my noble queen," Simon answered quietly, "I only wished for the money."

"Money is a poor excuse," Charlotte stated.

"If I may, my queen?" Peter asked, stepping forward.

Charlotte nodded for him to continue.

Peter set his gaze on Simon and began, "Simon, I must confess I am deeply disappointed in you. You were extremely loyal to the Crown until now. Why is that?"

"Like I said, Lord Peter," Simon replied. "It was because of money." He hung his head further down. "It was a stupid choice. I admit I was a fool. I deserve the punishment I will be given."

"Who persuaded you to do such a thing?" Peter inquired.

"Lord Cromwell. He pushed me to ally myself with Lord Tybalt. I didn't know what that would entail. All I thought about was the money and how it was better than what I received as a squire."

Charlotte's rage began to mount. "And that's what made you commit treason? A worthless thing like money?"

She stalked away from the disheartened boy. She spun to face him again. "I cannot ignore your act of treason. I must punish you and I will. I have no intention of postponing the punishment either. I will sentence you today and carry out the punishment tomorrow."

Simon's shoulders slumped, "Do as you must, my queen."

"The punishment for treason is death. You will be hanged for your crime. Your hanging will be conducted tomorrow at dawn."

Simon's head shot up and his eyes widened. The guilt was quickly replaced with panic. Peter apparently recognized

Simon's shock and stepped forward. "My queen, is there no better way to punish such a young person? Perhaps not as intimidating?"

"The boy is nearly a man," Lord Geoffrey jumped in. "He should be punished by the law."

"I agree with Lord Geoffrey," Lord Edmund replied.

The other knights murmured their agreement. Charlotte looked down at Simon's desperate state. She steeled herself from turning soft. She must think of Aurum and its safety. She shook her head, "I will not allow treason in my kingdom, Lord Peter. In this matter, I side with the other nobles. Squire Simon hangs tomorrow."

Simon threw his hand upward in pleading, "Please, your Majesty, have mercy on me! I give my word to never to do such a thing again. I only ask you for a second chance. Spare my life, I beg you, most glorious one!"

Charlotte remained solid. "No. You have threatened me and my kingdom. The price for that act is death."

"Please, my queen! Your most royal and radiant Highness, I beg of you to have mercy!" Simon pleaded.

"No!" Charlotte berated. "You deserve no such thing! You will no longer torment my kingdom."

Simon's head fell to the floor as he replied, "My queen, please..."

"Hold a moment, Simon," Lord Peter said, placing a hand on the lad's shoulder. Peter gave Charlotte his complete attention. "My queen, could you not consider Simon's words? Perhaps think of a less brutal punishment?"

"Lord Peter," Lord Edmund came in, "I understand your want for keeping a fellow squire alive. You've trained with him since he became a squire. But you cannot decide his fate. Only a king or queen may have this power. Her Majesty has spoken and condemned Squire Simon to death and so be it."

"Lord Edmund is correct, Lord Peter," Sir Randolph butted in. "The boy must pay for his mistakes."

Agreement rang through the gathering.

———————

Peter stared at his instructor and the rest of the lords in silence. They were willing to kill a boy no older than seventeen. Peter stared down at Simon. Sympathy filled Peter as he gazed down at his young friend. This was certainly not Simon's plan for his life. In Peter's mind, Simon was too young to hang. But the law overruled his thoughts. A man who committed treason must be hanged or beheaded. His gaze returned to Charlotte's cold eyes. Despite the hard wall protecting her every emotion, Peter could tell she was battling to keep them under control. She kept flicking her gaze from Simon, to the other lords and knights, and finally to him.

Peter spoke again, hoping she would listen to his reasoning, "Isn't there any other way to punish him?"

Her answer rather surprised him. "What would you suggest, Lord Peter? I cannot let him go without severe punishment."

"Let him be kept under watch until you return from your battle. Have him spend time in the dungeon, have him work as a servant, have him prove his loyalty by having him remain a squire for longer, but don't put him to death. Allow him a second chance. He may even be of use providing us with information concerning Lord Tybalt. In the end, I assure you that you will not regret your show of mercy." Peter took a deep breath when he finished, allowing his suggestions to sink into his fellow peers and Charlotte.

Charlotte sent her cold gaze down to Simon's slumped form. She seemed to be contemplating Peter's advice. Finally her green eyes were back on Peter. "I will leave off the hanging for now," she announced. "But," she added, "I will not release him from his death sentence until I have thought through the matter more carefully. I can agree to letting him remain under watch here. When I return home, I will decide his fate."

Peter nodded, "Very well. I give you my agreement on that matter."

Charlotte turned to the other nobles, "Will that satisfy you all?"

"It is as you say, my queen," Lord Edmund said. The others murmured the noble's response.

Peter breathed a sigh of relief. Charlotte would let Simon live. For now.

"Take the prisoner back to his tent, keep him bound, and post guards by his doors, for I still do not trust him," Charlotte ordered.

Peter watched as Simon got to his feet and Sir Richard and Sir Henry came to stand on either side of him. "May I say one more thing, my queen?" Simon asked, hope ringing in his voice.

"Speak then," Charlotte demanded.

"Your Majesty cannot possibly starve Lord Tybalt out. He has provisions that may last years if need be."

"Impossible," Charlotte replied. "How could he possibly have provisions to last years?"

"I don't know how such a thing is possible, but it is," Simon said, shaking his head.

"How do you know that Lord Tybalt has such numerous provisions?" Charlotte questioned.

"I overheard some of Lord Tybalt's knights bragging a few weeks back about how many provisions the feudal lord had in case of a siege," Simon answered.

Charlotte didn't respond. She only jerked her head for the two knights to take Simon back to his tent. After they had left, Charlotte announced, "I want us to prepare to lay siege to Lord Tybalt's fortress. We've waited long enough. I will no longer tolerate the lord's presence. He is a threat and must be killed."

"How, my queen?" Lord Edmund asked in confusion. "We have only half the mechanical weapons we need. We could very well lose."

"But perhaps Squire Simon is lying about Lord Tybalt's provisions, my queen?" Sir Randolph butted in. "He could easily be lying just to destroy our forces and do away with us permanently."

"Simon would do no such thing," Peter countered. "He wouldn't lie right after being given a second chance."

"Besides," Charlotte came in, "we won't lose. I have a weapon that Lord Tybalt could never imagine even existed."

"What, my queen?" Lord Geoffrey asked in curiosity.

"A phoenix."

"Of course," Peter thought. They would have the phoenix on their side. No one would be able to withstand the intensity of the creatures flames.

"Queen Charlotte!" an anxious voice cried out. A squire around fourteen ran headlong into the queen's tent, without an invitation. Peter caught the boy by his shoulders and shook him furiously.

"Never barge into the queen's quarters without permission, boy," Peter said angrily. "Have you lost your mind?"

The boy took deep breathes and bowed, "My apologies, my lord. I didn't think." The lad kept taking deep long breathes to steady his breathing. Out of nowhere, the boy's eyes widened in fright.

Peter caught sight of a dagger in Charlotte's hand. He breathed a sigh of relief for catching the boy before he met a dagger at his throat. Had Peter not been here, there was no telling what Charlotte would have done.

"What is so important to barge into my tent uninvited?" Charlotte asked, annoyance playing on every word she spoke.

"I tried to stop it, my queen, I really did. But..." the boy doubled over and began to take deep breathes again.

"What?" Peter asked.

The boy returned to a standing position and looked at the queen hesitantly before saying, "The phoenix, my queen and Lord Peter."

"What about the phoenix?" Charlotte demanded.

"The phoenix, Your Majesty, is gone."

Chapter 20

"I'm going, Peter. That's final," Charlotte said again, as she strapped the remaining leather to Luna's chest. She looked up from her finished work to Peter's defeated expression. Yesterday, she had announced that they would be attacking Lord Tybalt's fortress, while she searched out the phoenix. It was her way of making up for her foolishness for leaving the giant bird in unexperienced hands. She had been the cause for the bird to flee, so she must find it.

"I'm going with you then," Peter replied, reaching for a saddle resting on one of the horse's stalls.

Charlotte planted herself in his path, "No, Peter. I need you here. You must help lead the men into battle alongside General Wymer and Sir Randolph."

"They won't need my help," Peter argued. "I would be of much more use to you being with you."

Charlotte knew his motive for coming. He wanted her safe. Sometimes she didn't understand why he wouldn't let her travel around alone. Ever since the ambush attack, he had paid closer attention to where she went and if she went outside the camp he would make sure to tag along or send someone else to look after her. Peter's extra consideration for her was growing annoying at times. She needed to convince him that she could look after herself. She had been doing so since she was young. "I understand you want to keep me safe. But you will be more useful to me here with the attack."

Peter pressed on, "What if something happens to you? Lord Tybalt could still have men waiting to ambush you."

"I am quite safe with Luna. Plus, I have a sword and dagger," she replied, patting her weapons tied around her waist.

Peter let out a defeated sigh, "Then I won't go on arguing about the matter. I see I'm not needed."

Charlotte watched him turn to leave, his disappointment in the air around her. She hurried after him and confronted him, "Peter, wait."

He looked down at her, his blue eyes reflecting signs of hope. "Yes?"

"I understand your caution about letting me go out alone, especially after what happened two weeks ago. But please," she implored, putting a hand on his shoulder, "you must realize I can fend for myself."

"I've known you could care for yourself from the day I met you in Vetitum Wood," Peter answered. "I just don't like the idea of letting you travel alone through enemy territory."

"I'm not heading into enemy territory. I'm going back through Black-fire Wood. I'm going back to where we first found the phoenix."

"I assumed you would," Peter said. "But, Charlotte, Lord Tybalt's men could be anywhere. You give me your word that you'll remain safe."

"I will be fine, Peter," Charlotte reassured. "This is my responsibility and now you must do yours. Help lead the troops into battle."

"I will do my best," Peter answered. His hand slipped into hers, injecting warmth into her body. "I promise."

The rising mist of dawn gave Malum Wood an even more foreboding look. The heavy fog along with the dark morning, gave Peter and the rest of the men cover for readying the weapons and aligning the men for attack.

"There are a great number of guards, Lord Peter," General Wymer said in a whisper.

Peter forced himself to answer calmly. No need to panic. Panic is useless on the battlefield. "If we keep low in the fog they will not see us," Peter whispered back. "Are your men assembled?"

"Yes," answered General Wymer. "Sir Richard and Sir Henry are waiting for the command to move forward."

Peter turned to Sir Randolph on the other side of him, "What happens if there are too many men. Will we retreat?"

"We will never retreat until we have won," Sir Randolph declared.

"Of course," Peter responded through a deep breath.

Sir Randolph must have heard Peter's nervousness, for he slapped him on the back reassuringly, "Have faith, Lord Peter. General Wymer knows how to defeat an enemy and

Queen Charlotte knew what she was doing sending us to lead an assault. All we do is fight alongside the general and obey Her Majesty."

Peter's mind went to Charlotte at the mention of her name. He had promised to do his best on the field of battle. He must do his best. He would do it. He must think of Aurum's and Charlotte's protection. Peter nodded to General Wymer, "Tell your men to start bombarding the fortress with Mangonels."

Charlotte soared through the air riding Luna. She scanned the ground, looking for specific landmarks she could identify that led to the phoenix's cavern. It was near noon and Peter and the men were most likely inside the walls. The army had started bombarding Lord Tybalt's walls at dawn. Hopefully by now the men were weakening the enemy. But she knew deep down that if she failed to find and bring back the phoenix they would be defeated. The prophecy had stated that in it's poetic form of writing. She only hoped Peter could hold off the enemy long enough to get the giant bird back.

"Lord Peter! The walls are down!" Sir Randolph shouted over the rumbling noise of thundering rocks.

"You're in charge from here on out!" Peter shouted back. "What do you want our men to do?"

"General Wymer has already sent his troops forward," his instructor yelled to him. "After he tires Lord Tybalt's forces, we'll come in with a fresh new group."

Through the darkness Peter could make out the fortress' walls crumbling to nothing but rubble. The noise echoed in his ears and the falling stone sent the earth shaking. The wind from the stone's impact whipped across Peter's face. Suddenly, he felt himself slip into memories of his own castle siege. Lord Roger had led a siege against Peter's fortress when he was a newly made lord. Peter had lost, forcing him to surrender his beloved fortress. Thankfully, in the end, Charlotte had given it back to him in return for his services in the battle against Morgana.

"Let us proceed, Lord Peter," Sir Randolph announced, shaking Peter from his memories. He remembered Sir Randolph saying that the attackers of a siege had higher advantage when supplied with the right material and the correct number of men. If there was one thing he learned from his castle being under siege, it was that to every clever trick the defenders played to increase their safety, there was an equally clever offense. Peter knew they didn't have nearly as much material as needed, but he and the rest would be fighting for something they could not dare to lose. They would be fighting for their kingdom. He would be fighting for the kingdom and its queen. He wouldn't back down from the battle until he saw Lord Tybalt raise a white flag. Peter started forward.

"Hold a moment, Lord Peter," Sir Randolph said, catching him by the shoulders.

"What is it, Sir Randolph?" Peter asked, anxious to charge straight into the fortress and demand a surrender.

"While my men charge into the bailey, I want you to go directly into the Keep. Lord Tybalt's Keep is in a vulnerable position and will be easy to get to without drawing attention."

"Why mustn't I help you?" Peter asked in confusion. "Half of those men are under my care."

"Because I want you to find Lord Tybalt yourself and face him alone," Sir Randolph answered.

At first, Peter was shocked at his instructor's orders. He wanted Peter to find Lord Tybalt himself? "Are you sure? Do you not want someone more experienced to go after the lord?"

"No," Sir Randolph replied, "I know how important this is to you. Your queen is in danger because of him. You deserve to face him yourself."

"She's not my queen, Sir Randolph," Peter answered. For once he was thankful for the darkness that shielded his reddening face.

"Another thing," Sir Randolph said. "If you come back victorious I will tell the queen you are ready to become a knight."

Shock was replaced with excitement at the mention of his knight's ceremony. The last time his instructor had spoken of his ceremony was nearly a month ago. Peter had grown to think his instructor had forgotten. Perhaps he hadn't. Perhaps he had been waiting for the right moment. Peter stood taller, "Then I will do as you say."

Sir Randolph chuckled, "Then go. If you beat his lordship I daresay you will become a knight in no time and perhaps even win the queen's affections."

Peter shook his head, "No such thing will happen, Sir Randolph. Queen Charlotte has made it clear she wishes to rule alone. No man will ever sit on the throne in her realm."

"I think that will change," Sir Randolph said. "I've been observing her when she is with you. She seems to trust you and accept you as a friend. That could grow into something more." Sir Randolph nudged Peter forward, "Now go."

Peter went after the rest of the men who were charging the fort. When he stepped inside, he immediately surveyed the grounds before him. The earth was littered with the slain. Blood was splattered over the ground and walls. A fire was raging through the Auxiliary and countless men were in hand to hand combat.

Peter caught sight of the Keep and raced across the clearing for the building. The second he reached the stairs to the inside, a man blocked his path. Peter recognized him as the guard from Charlotte's rescue attempt. The man charged at Peter. Peter swerved and knocked the man down with the flat end of his blade. After seeing his enemy had fallen, Peter threw open the Keep's doors and stepped inside. Surprise welcomed him when he noticed no guards standing by the doors. Normally, there would be at least two standing watch.

Peter looked around and caught sight of the staircase that led up to where Charlotte had been held. Peter started towards the stairs. Something deep down inside told him he would find the evil lord close to where Charlotte had been held captive. He ran up the narrow, dark stairs, meeting an occasional adversary here and there. To his advantage, Peter didn't encounter many. Lord Tybalt must have sent most of them outside. But, to his disadvantage, he was climbing up the stairs with his sword hand to the wall. Also, the stairs were full of cracks and dents, causing Peter to trip and lose his balance on occasion. But, no matter how hard it was, he'd reach the top. Because Charlotte's and Aurum's future depended on it.

He stepped onto the highest floor and surveyed the dimly lit hallway. He could feel his conscience pulling him towards a heavy wooden door with rusty metal hinges. He started towards the doorway, each step telling him he was closer and closer to meeting the lord who had started all of this. Peter shook the door with its rusty handle. It rattled on its hinges; it didn't seem to be locked. Strange. Treading with caution, Peter pushed on the handles. The door creaked open with a loud squeaking noise, revealing a dimly lit room with a single chair. The room held a musty scent and offered little light except for the stray candle on the wall. When Peter's eyes had adjusted to the darker room, he caught sight of a shadowy figure standing in the darkness. The figure had his sword drawn.

Chapter 21

"Lord Peter," the shadow hissed, "I've been waiting."

Peter looked at the figure skeptically, "You know who I am?"

The shadow nodded, "Lord Cromwell has told me much about you."

Peter nodded, acknowledging the noble's name, "Lord Cromwell."

"He told me you were dangerous and not to be trusted," the figure went on. "It appears he was right, for he is dead."

Peter pointed his sword at the dark shadow. "I'm only dangerous when someone threatens something I have to defend. You threaten someone I vowed to protect. In doing so, you have made me your enemy."

The shadow let out an evil snicker and began to approach Peter. "I'm not Lord Cromwell or that insolent boy, Lord Peter. I won't be easily done away with. As you probably know, I'm not afraid to kill in order to receive what I want."

Peter readied himself for an attack, "And I, my lord, am not afraid to end your life in order to protect someone I have come to care for a great deal. I won't back down like some might. You've met your match with me, Lord Tybalt."

At that moment, their swords clashed.

———

Charlotte circled around the cave atop of Luna's back, in preparation to land. She could only hope that the phoenix lay inside and she could get it back in time to help Peter.

Luna landed near the stream and allowed Charlotte to slip to the ground. She took a deep breath to focus and relax, then started towards the water cave's dark entrance.

———

The weight of heavy metal crashed against Peter's sword as he struggled to ward off Lord Tybalt's blows. In the dim room it was difficult to see the other noble. His attacks seemed to come out of nowhere, giving Peter hardly any time to defend and certainly no time to perform a counterattack. Right now he was trying his best to prevent himself from getting injured. It didn't take Peter long to figure out Lord Tybalt wouldn't be easy to defeat. The banished lord had a series of advantages. On top of being stronger than Peter, Lord Tybalt seemed perfectly content on battling in an enclosed room. It was almost as if the noble was used to such combats. On the contrary, Peter was inept at fighting indoors. He had alway trained and fought outdoors. The enclosed space made Peter feel uneasy. Each time he moved he had to take care not to let Lord Tybalt corner him.

But, as they continued to battle, Peter began to notice a change in Lord Tybalt's blows. Whenever one hit Peter's sword, the more wearisome the noble seemed to become. While Peter was fresh and full of boiling energy for only having to defend himself. Finally, he came to a conclusion. Peter would let Lord Tybalt wear himself out. Then, Peter would use all his force to bring the evil noble down.

Charlotte rested her hand on the phoenix's beak. The creature's bright yellow eyes were fixed intently on Charlotte. Making sure the beast would follow, Charlotte began to wade back towards the cave's entrance. Instead of following her, the giant bird let out a screech of rage and tore away from Charlotte's outstretched hand. Charlotte retracted her palm and ducked out of reach from the bird's whipping tail. The phoenix sailed out of her reach and landed on a large branch jutting out from the ceiling. Only when the bird was still did Charlotte notice the gash in the bird's thigh. Fury started to bubble in Charlotte. No wonder the phoenix had flown off. Someone had evidently not liked the bird and punished it. Blood was dripping from the large wound in strange colors of yellow, orange, and red. The same colors as its feathers. Whenever the phoenix tried to move, the blood would rush from the gash, falling in fiery colors into the pool below.

Charlotte put a hand to her head and rubbed her eyes. There was no denying the fact. The bird was injured. How in all the world would she get it to fly to the battlefield, let alone fight with an injury that size? Charlotte groped for an idea. She needed to find a solution, fast, or risk seeing her kingdom reduced to nothing but ashes.

———————

Sweat poured down Peter's face and into his eyes, blinding him. He blinked, struggling to rid the moisture from his sight. His strategy of tiring Lord Tybalt into defeat wasn't going according to plan. After what seemed like hours of having been hacked at, Peter was growing weary. There was no telling how much more he could endure. If something didn't happen fast, he could very well collapse in exhaustion.

Lord Tybalt took another swing at Peter's neck. Peter ducked and, taking advantage of being on the floor, swung at Lord Tybalt's legs. Lord Tybalt stepped out of reach with a growl, making Peter take notice of the new cut he had given the other noble. Peter jumped up just in time to see Lord Tybalt charging at him. Peter veered to the left and smacked the angry noble on the back with the flat of his blade. In fury Lord Tybalt swung around and attacked Peter with swift hacks. Peter struggled to cover up as the blows came from every direction. Out of nowhere, a hard, pointed, object struck him in the gut, causing him to double over in pain. Bringing himself to his knees, Peter tried to refocus and make out what had stabbed him. He could hear Lord Tybalt's evil laughter from above. Looking up, he noticed the banished lord's sword hilt hovering close by. So that's what had struck him. Peter felt his stomach for blood but found none, other than the blood from his enemies. Forcing himself to ignore his throbbing abdomen, Peter stood to his full height and said through gritted teeth, "We aren't finished, Lord Tybalt."

"Oh? We're not?" Lord Tybalt taunted. "You look finished to me."

Peter was about to reply when a thundering rumble came from outside. The stone walls began to quake and tremble and the sudden smell of smoke filled the musty air. Peter felt an unusual amount of heat travel across his skin and he began to realize how hot and stuffy the tower room had become. The walls and floors began to crack under the quaking pressure and heat. Peter surveyed the room in alarm, unsure of what was happening. There was no weapon that could do such damage at once. It was impossible. Unless... A thought came to Peter's mind. Charlotte. The phoenix. That's what could cause so much destruction. Charlotte must have found the giant bird and succeeded in bringing it back.

Lord Tybalt's eyes were wide with fright as he gazed around the crumbling tower. "No," he began to whisper. Turning to Peter his eyes narrowed and he roared, "No!" The furious lord charged at Peter in complete madness.

Bracing himself, Peter blocked Lord Tybalt's blow, knocked it aside with one swift swing, and drove his own blade into the noble's stomach.

———————

Charlotte watched as the prophecy was fulfilled. The Keep's walls were ablaze with the phoenix's fire. After lighting the towering fortress, the giant beast had disappeared. Perhaps never to be seen again for another hundred years just as the legend said. As the stones began to fall with terrifying speed, Charlotte's thoughts immediately went out to Peter. She hadn't seen him among the dead, which brought hope that he was alive. But if he somehow happened to be in the Keep, there was not much of a chance of him escaping the burning building.

She shivered at her own memories of the village fire. She hadn't managed to escape the hungry flames. She would forever bear the fire's mark on her arms and back. The burns left their mark on her and her life permanently.

A figure emerged from the Keep's smoking entrance and stumbled towards her. He was covered in soot and blood was matted on his armor and chainmail. A fresh cut glistened near his right eye. Only when he reached her did she recognize him. Peter. She approached her companion and looked up into his blue eyes.

"It's finished, Charlotte," he informed. "Lord Tybalt is dead. You are safe once again."

Chapter 22

Peter walked down the torch-lit hallway to the Great Hall, heading towards his knighting ceremony. With the help of a younger squire, his armor had been cleaned and shined until the metal shone under the lights. His sword had been sharpened and buffed till it was shimmering.

Peter blinked and shook his head inside his helmet. After going through the traditional ritual of spending the night at the nearby cathedral praying and fasting through the night, he struggled not to succumb to the overpowering desire to sleep.

He approached the Keep's doors and two servants opened them for him, revealing the richly decorated Great Hall. The large room was full of nobles and their ladies looking at him in admiration. Peter continued down the aisle taking in the people around him. The Lords of the Council stood near the ends of the rows, nodding their encouragement. Not far from them Simon stood, smiling at him. The squire mouthed a quick 'thank you' and Peter understood. After the battle, Charlotte had released her charges of hanging Simon if the boy would stay on longer as a squire for a punishment. Sir Randolph stood next to Simon, smiling in approval at Peter.

A wash of sadness swept over Peter as he surveyed the people around him as he walked. There were three people he had wanted here for his ceremony. His father, King Philip, and Godfrey. His dream was to make his father proud and become a knight to King Philip's army. Now, neither were here to see him. He tore his gaze from the smiling faces and back to the front of the Hall. All thoughts of his father, King Philip, and Godfrey left him as he stared in wonder at the queen before her throne. A crown of sparkling gold and silver rested on her head. Her flowing dark hair fell down to her waist. Her slim figure was wrapped in a gown of shining silver along with glimmering gems on her bellowing sleeves. A sword of the finest quality was folded in between her hands by her side against the floor. Peter was grateful for the helmet that hid his face, for he surely must be gaping. She was beautiful.

Peter approached Charlotte's throne and stood before her, bowed, and waited for her approval to kneel. Through his helmet he saw the young queen's painted lips curve into a smile.

"Do you wish me to continue, Sir Randolph?" Charlotte asked in her authoritative voice.

Sir Randolph called out, pride in every word he spoke, "Proceed, my great queen, for he is ready."

Charlotte nodded and turned her attention back to Peter. "Kneel, Squire Peter," she ordered.

He did as he was told. Charlotte withdrew her sword from its sheath and held the flat end of the blade above Peter's right shoulder. In a loud voice she began the knight's oath, "Do not be fearful of your enemies. Remain brave and righteous so that God's love may shine on you. Always tell the truth even if death threatens you. Protect and fight for the innocent and commit no wrong. That is your oath, Sir Peter." She brought the sword's flat blade down on both of Peter's shoulders. "Arise, a knight to the kingdom of Aurum."

Peter arose to a standing position and applause erupted from the audience. He bowed in deep veneration to Charlotte and said to her alone, "Charlotte, I promise to protect you and Aurum till the day I die."

She responded with a nod and a sweet smile, then turned her gaze to the cheering crowd. Peter turned around and faced the smiling faces and cheers of approval. He surveyed the room. This was the land he was born to serve. These were the people he would defend. He glanced at Charlotte standing next to him. This was the queen he had come to love. He would protect it all even if he must sacrifice his own life. Nothing would ever threaten Queen Charlotte's realm while he was its protector.

Made in the USA
Middletown, DE
11 January 2020